THE COMTESSE OF MIDNIGHT

BY ALINA K. FIELD

ISBN No. 978-1-944063-34-4
Havenlock Press
PO Box 1891
La Mirada, CA 90637-1891

February 15, 2022
Previously Published in *Storm & Shelter: a Bluestocking Belles Collection with Friends*, April 13, 2021.

This is a work of fiction. Names, characters, places, and incidents either are the product of the author's imagination or are used fictitiously, and any resemblance to actual persons, living or dead, business establishments, events, or locales is entirely coincidental.

Cover Design by Melody Barber

A Scottish Earl on a quest for the elusive Comtesse de Fontenay, rescues a French lady smuggler during a devastating storm, taking shelter with her. As the stormy night drags on, he suspects she knows the lady he's seeking, the lady who holds the secret to his identity. When she admits she herself is the Comtesse Fontenay, just not the one he's seeking, she dashes all his hopes—and promises him new ones.

Originally published in
Storm & Shelter:
a Bluestocking Belles Collection with Friends

Dedication

For Romance Readers Everywhere!

CHAPTER ONE

A Smuggler on the Beach

Malcolm Comyn gripped the reins and clamped his other hand to his hat as a gust of horizontal rain shot straight from the North Sea.

Damnation. The rain struck like pellets of ice blasted from a shotgun.

The gelding he'd borrowed from the White Hart in Blythburgh snorted and ducked his head. A sure-footed animal, he'd managed the journey north on the coast road and then inland on Maresrow Road briskly enough. That was before they reversed course to head east again, back to the coast road. The worst of the rainstorm had caught up with them and now, the poor fellow flagged, picking his way along the verge of the flooded road.

"Soon, lad," he told the steady beast. But a few minutes more and they'd turn north and head onward to Lowestoft,

His morning mission a failure, he'd decided to push on to the Blue Boar where he could wait out the storm while puzzling out his next step. *If* they could make it, and he prayed they could. They'd passed no public lodgings on the morning ride. They would just have to plunge ahead.

Three weeks he'd been searching, to no avail. 'Twas now the first day of April, the country in uproar over grain costs and Bonaparte's escape, the weather gods wrathful as well. There'd be no hurrying back to London, neither by land nor by sea, even if he wished to give up his quest for the woman. And he didn't.

And he wouldn't.

At the end of Maresrow Road, he steered his mount left. The road north climbed above the marshes, traversing sheer cliffs that to his right loomed above a raging sea. To his left, a manor perched atop a slight rise, lights gleaming in the sparkling windows.

Hope sparked and just as quickly died. This manor house could not be his destination. Bloodmoor Hill Manor was not on the coastal road. He might stop here and seek directions, or even shelter.

On the other hand, making inquiries of the local gentry might raise more questions from them than he was willing to answer. Better to pick the brain of another publican or passing travelers in a cozy tap room.

Though it must still be afternoon, the churning clouds darkened the sky to late evening, and the rain sheeted the path ahead. He rode on in the diminishing light, his mount growing twitchier and twitchier. Squinting, he pulled up on the reins.

His heart pounded fiercely. The coast road ahead, the road that led to Lowestoft and shelter, had completely vanished.

"Steady boy," he said, more for himself than for the good-humored gelding. Had he put his horse into a gallop, he'd have ridden straight into the abyss, traversing that road where it now lay, hundreds of feet below on the rocky beach. Traversing it as a ghost, as 'twas sure that he'd be dead. The matter of who was the rightful Earl of Menteith would be settled.

Damn, but wouldn't that fit his enemy's plan to a tee?

Another bone-rattling sheet of rain pelted him. The full force of his predicament overcame him, and he let out a stream of oaths. Today's quest for Bloodmoor Hill Manor had been another fool's errand. With no sure direction, he might have missed the road; he might have passed directly by an overgrown lane leading to the manor.

Or the manor might be a phantasm of someone's imagination, or, more likely, a false lead planted by the villain plaguing him.

"What now?" he asked aloud.

The horse looked back at him with a snort.

"I'm as miserable as ye are, fellow. Come. Let's find the both of us shelter."

Turning back south, he eyed the lighted windows of the lonely manor. Asking for shelter there was an option.

But a branch of the coastal road continued south, and he recalled that, at the intersection with Maresrow Road, a stone post had stood, leaning as if pushed by the sea winds. He hadn't bothered to read the name carved upon it. He rode on, hoping to find a nearby village, preferably one with an inn. He would make one last foray for anonymous shelter before inquiring at the manor.

His mount stalled abruptly, ears flicking. A shout and an equine squeal carried on the wind, the animal's cry mixing with the crashing of waves. This distance south of the cliffs, the road fronted a field that sloped gently to a rocky beach studded with boulders. A beached vessel rested there with figures circling around it, their shouts carrying his way.

He nudged the gelding off the road. The beast tediously picked his way through the gorse, and boulders, and rain-induced streams, whilst Malcolm prayed that the ground would hold.

Finally reaching the beach, he saw white cloth puddled around the broken mast of the small sloop. A train of laden donkeys stumbled off to the north, two men guiding their precarious steps, whilst another man remained behind. He disappeared under sailcloth and came out with a cask, depositing it on the rocky shore. The wind swirled and sent a wave that threatened to claim the cargo, and the man dove for it, scooting it higher on the beach.

These were free traders, and this was a foolish one to battle Neptune over a cask of spirits. The next wave could very well take him as well as the cargo.

"Halloo," Malcolm called.

The man scrambled to his feet. Short and slight, his oilcloth coat tented over him. He was otherwise dripping wet, a knit cap clinging down to his eyebrows.

He dove under the sail again and came back with another cask.

Either he hadn't heard or he was ignoring the greeting. "Do you need help?" Malcolm called.

The man spun around, a scowl on his young face, and shook his head.

Another wave swamped him, the sea tugging at his boots and legs. He fell back, unsteady and struggling against the pull of the wave, still clutching his cargo.

Malcolm dismounted, tossed the reins around a stout boulder, and waded into the surf. He reached a hand and pulled the delicate lad up, swept the cask out of his loosening grip, and fought his way back up the beach with the lad in tow.

Eyes flashed up at him. Gray, or green, or blue—the color was uncertain in this dim light, but the lashes framing them were long, the lips full, the face a smooth heart shape filled with annoyance.

Feminine annoyance.

He swept a gaze over the coats and trousers, confirming the curves below. Almost confirming.

And if confirmed, it would be the first bit of intrigue unrelated to his earldom that he'd had in months.

He whisked the smuggler up under his free arm, swallowing a chuckle, ignoring the unmistakably female howl of protest.

***

Merde. With fingers numb from fighting the storm, holding onto the casks was proving nigh impossible. And the man oughtn't to be here.

The hand reaching out was large, the arm it was attached to a strong one, and the stranger was a full head taller. He wasn't a revenue agent though, or not a known one. They'd all be snug in their beds in a storm like this, which is where the crew would be very soon. As soon as the men stowed the barrels and the landlord of the Queen's Barque received this delivery.

The man was not with the government, yet his scrutiny was a close one.

"Nooo." The scold came unbidden because he'd plucked a body tight up against him, juggling the cask in his other arm.

The devil he was, and too damned presumptuous. "Put me down. You oughtn't to be here. Go see to your horse. The animal will have the reins free in moments."

"Ungrateful brat." Still cradling the cask, he slogged back to the horse, soothing the creature with a gentle touch that quite impressed. Except, that he still held the cask that wasn't his.

"You. That's mine."

"Aye, and I'm carryin' it for ye. Come." He beckoned. "Get yourself out of the surf."

That was probably wise. Whether the sloop would be there in the morning was anyone's guess. A pity that. Nothing about this run had been easy.

This was usually a task for the midnight hour, completed by dawn. But the storm had changed everything. They were lucky to be alive.

"That cask is mine, and I'll have it now."

He picked up the other one. "I'll carry the both. Ye'll lead the horse."

The beast rolled his eyes and snorted with only mild annoyance. This was a fine creature to be only a bit discomposed by his day's work and the weather.

"Fine, then. I will lead him."

When the man turned with the casks and stomped off toward the embankment a sharp whistle checked him.

"Not that way. We will follow the beach. It will be faster and less treacherous than taking that hillside."

"Aye. Unless a wee wave comes and sweeps us away. And where would it be that we're going?"

And there it was, a guess before, but now, *certainement*: a Scots accent, one that sent a slither of fear up the spine. And why would *another* finely dressed Scotsman be visiting these parts?

Courage. "I am going as far as the village. Then you may give me my casks, and I will give you your horse, and you may go your own way."

"There's a village?" he asked.

"Yes, but of course. Fenwick on Sea." A sweet outpost of decent people in this pitiless land. "You are a stranger, I see." The crew had seen many strange people descending on Fenwick-on-Sea seeking refuge from the weather. It was wise to be wary of strangers. "Where are you coming from? Scotland?"

He blinked. "Not as far as all that. I've traveled from Blythburgh."

"And where were you going today that you didn't know of Fenwick-on-Sea?"

He quirked a lip. Water poured off the brim of his hat and coursed over a strong nose and firm jaw, yet he looked of a sudden incredibly cheerful.

"If you are thinking to take up trading in these parts—"

"No." He shook his head, spraying water like Hector, the great beast of a dog that guarded the village inn. "I'm seeking shelter, for me and for this poor fellow. Is there an inn in this village?"

How inconvenient. They were seeking the same destination. Nevertheless, seeing a horse suffer was unbearable.

"Most certainly there is an inn. The Queen's Barque."

They walked on in silence for a time, reaching the part of the beach that flowed into the road that became the village's Market Street. Already lights gleamed in the windows of the inn and the village's other shops and cottages, though it was likely not yet five of the clock.

They stopped at the entrance to the inn's courtyard. He might lead his horse and enter there.

"Give me my casks now, and I'll be on my way." The casks were better carried through the stable entrance and left in the brewhouse for the spirits to be let down.

He eyed the lighted windows of the inn. "It looks to be crowded. I can sleep in the stable if need be. Where are you taking these?"

That question was better ignored. "A gentleman who'll sleep in a stable? Hah."

He turned away from the inn and moved closer. Too close. "A lady who'll smuggle gin?" His lips stretched into a slow grin that matched his teasing tone.

There was no point correcting him, and anyway, Marielle Plessiers was almost to the end of her ruse. Once the casks were delivered, she, like the men in the crew, would disappear, and eventually find the way home. This weather would not continue forever.

And this one... Yes, he was handsome, and he knew it. And he was younger than she'd first thought, certainly younger than herself, and likely to think himself a stallion in bed. Young handsome men were a rarity in her world, and the ones she'd encountered could never be trusted. As for the bed skills... pah. The Comte de Fontenay had taught her to be skeptical of men bragging too much.

"It is not gin. It is a very fine brandy. Now be the gentleman you appear to be and give me my casks."

"Come along. I assume these are for the innkeeper. Perhaps they'll help me negotiate a better bed than the hayloft."

She ought to crack open his thick Scottish head.

He turned to enter the inn's courtyard. Spluttering, she hurried to catch up, and grabbed his arm. "Not this way." She yanked him along to the stable entrance.

CHAPTER TWO

The Queen's Barque

Malcolm swallowed a chuckle and went along like a dutiful packhorse. In the stable yard, carriages and wagons crowded the cobbled space. A groom hailed them and ran out, eying him closely before shifting his gaze back to the lady.

"We were *that* worried," he said.

She gave her head a little shake. "This man is looking for shelter."

A boy raced out and joined the other fellow. "You can't mean me to saddle your mare," he cried. "The coast road is gone."

She chewed her luscious lip.

"He's right," Malcolm said. "I was headed that way. The whole road is at the bottom of the cliff. With the rain falling this hard, I wouldn't risk trying to go around through the marshland."

She shrugged. "I see. Well, I mustn't subject the dear girl to this weather. Please see that this fellow is dry and well fed." She handed over the reins.

"And fetch me the bag attached to my saddle." Malcolm turned to the lady. "And where do these go?"

She rolled her eyes and led Malcolm over to the covered carriageway that led to the inn's courtyard.

A tall, lean man popped out of the inn door, followed by a woman in an apron. She scurried behind the building, but the man crossed the courtyard and joined them. Mayhap this anxious looking fellow in shirtsleeves was the innkeeper.

"Thank heavens." He tucked a bar towel away in his waistband. "We were worried. Ryman." He beckoned the groom who'd first greeted them. "Take these."

Malcolm glanced at the lady smuggler, who nodded permission. He handed over the precious cargo.

The innkeeper cast Malcolm a curious glance, and then turned a questioning gaze on the lady.

"Mr. Brewster, this gentleman needs shelter."

"Every room is taken, m—"

A quick shake of her head coincided with the lad delivering his bag, both actions interrupting a declaration of her name.

Ah, well. More delicious mystery.

Brewster frowned and went on. "The road north is washed out. All the others are flooded. We've had castaways washed ashore.

There's talk of ships foundering at the point. The last carriage limped in only an hour ago. I've had to put the wounded in the south wing, despite the state it is in. The east wing is even worse."

"The stables will do," Malcolm said.

"It's overflowing with coachmen and grooms."

"Well then, if ye've a dry blanket, I'll take a bench in the taproom." Malcolm turned to the lady. "Allow me to buy ye dinner."

An indecipherable look passed over the landlord's face. "That won't do."

"Why not?" Perhaps there was a riding officer in the taproom. He wanted to hear the man say it.

He cleared his throat. "There's a, er, reporter hereabouts. From one of those London scandal sheets, the Teatime Tattler. Wife heard someone whispering about it. We don't know who it is."

A reporter for a scandal sheet? That was infinitely worse than a riding officer.

Three weeks of grueling travel and uncomfortable inns had him fighting unending fatigue. He'd been trying to get ahead of a looming scandal, one that threatened everything dear to him, including his very identity. He'd been undecided whether to publish the story himself or try to conceal it.

Damnation. He needed more time to finish his quest, more time to decide on the best course of action.

The lady pressed her lips together whilst the innkeeper stood silently. These villagers were a cagey lot. They guarded their tongues and, where the lady was concerned, names.

He must do the same—if anyone could smoke out a peer of the realm it was a London reporter.

"What of your ancient wing?" she asked.

"I've barely touched Maiden's Wing. Fixed the roof in the upper rooms, so they'll be dry, but... I'll need the revenue from that large south wing to do her up right."

"The Maiden's Wing," Malcolm mused. "After Bess, I presume."

"Aye, and dating to her visit here, and not much touched since. 'Twill be an elegant suite of rooms for distinguished visitors when we are finished."

"Are there lower rooms there?"

"Only one. It's our smallest wing. The ground floor has naught but a furnished parlor. But there's no bed."

He was damnably tired of the wet. "If there's a hearth and some fuel, you may bring in..." He glanced at the lady. She was dodging the scandalmongers as well. "You may bring in pallets for us, or at the very least, blankets."

She blinked, the flutter of feminine eyelashes a silent expression of discord. "Us?"

He paused, eyeing her. He wasn't a man given to whims, especially where women were concerned. And it might be a damned foolish thing, risking sleep in the same room with a woman who wore trousers and smuggled spirits. And then there'd been that robbery attempt by an ugly fellow at an inn outside Clacton-on-Sea.

On the other hand, she might know the way to Bloodmoor Hill Manor. And from what he could see, she was pretty.

"If there's only the one room available and no bed, we might as well share the parlor. I'm dead on my feet, mayhap ye are as well after your... exertions. I'll not molest ye, my word as a gentleman, and this good man as witness." He swallowed another chuckle. Given those casks of brandy, how good Brewster was might be in question. "And I also would rather not appear in some London tattle sheet." For he had a feeling, the lady was not some local smuggler's woman, but a lady of quality. He was going on gut instinct perhaps, or the tone of her speech, genteel with a hint of something foreign.

Or she could be a London ladybird retired to the sea coast. If he wasn't so bluidy tired, perhaps that would be all right.

Telling them to wait while he fetched the key, Brewster turned for the door. As he passed into the courtyard, they heard him bellow. "What're you doing here, Alice? There's rooms needing cleaning."

The aproned woman cast a curious glance his way. He sent her a challenging frown and turned away, the hair on his neck quivering. Nosy maids and scandal sheet scribes—the sooner he left the Queen's Barque, the better.

***

Key in hand, the lady led him through the courtyard, past the outbuilding she said was the brewhouse, around the back of the taproom and along another covered passage to a sagging door.

“Allow me.” The lock creaked and resisted, the metal threatening to bend. He mumbled a curse and tried again. This time the mechanism screeched and opened.

A stairway led up from the entry. To the right was another door, this one with no lock. When he pushed the door open, faint scurrying noises told him they wouldn’t be entirely alone. The room smelled of mice and damp but appeared dusty and otherwise reasonably clean. A table held the middle of the room with a few chairs placed neatly about, and near the fireplace was a threadbare sofa and two worn wing chairs, all upholstered in an aging brocade that might once have been striped in blue.

“It’s not as bad as I feared,” he said. “Ye may have the sofa.”

Her shrug was quite elegant. “It is used upon occasion by... local people. When the other parlors are taken,” she added.

It was used for stowing goods, in other words.

Not that he cared. The exploits of the free traders had naught to do with him, and having his own small distillery, he was no friend to the King’s gaugers.

“Do they also use the rooms above?”

"No."

"I'll just run up and make sure the ceiling won't fall in on us." And check that they truly were alone. Since seeing his cousin assaulted in London by paid thugs, and fending off that inn thief, he'd grown warier, if one didn't count the whole madness of this expedition.

And a night spent with a lady smuggler? The foolishness of it made him smile, but needs must. If she was less intriguing, he'd bump a coachman into the taproom and sleep with his horse.

Waving him away, she walked to the hearth where a lamp and tinderbox sat upon the mantel.

He pocketed the key and navigated the dark stairs carefully, making a quick survey of the upper rooms. The ceilings were streaked with water stains, and in various places, wood paneling had warped, but the buckets and tubs placed in strategic spots sat empty. The floors, and therefore the ceiling above the parlor seemed dry and solid enough. The bed ropes held no mattresses, and only a few scattered chairs and tables littered the rooms. Even the vermin might have abandoned this floor for the cozier regions below.

He reached the foot of the stairs just as Brewster arrived with a scuttle of coal, blankets, and two servants carrying buckets of hot water and a massive covered tray. The innkeeper left, promising to send over clean pallets.

A good thing, since the sofa might have other occupants nestling in the comfortable upholstery.

Eyes averted, the male servant silently went to work making a fire while the maid set out their dinner. When they'd left, Malcolm draped his damp overcoat on a chair and helped the lady out of her oilskin.

Underneath, she wore another coat that failed even more miserably than the oilskin at hiding her womanly figure.

"Your cap is soaking." His fingers itched to snatch it off of her head, to get a look at what was hidden there. "If you wish to remove it—"

"No," she said with enough haughtiness to pass for a duchess.

"Very well." He pulled out a chair for her, and she seated herself gracefully.

Uncertain about the appetite of a lady smuggler, he defaulted to good manners and filled a plate for her with lady-sized morsels. The innkeeper had provided enough food for two or three men, so perhaps lady smugglers didn't stint on their meals.

Outside, a howl rattled the window as the storm surged and grew fiercer, the rain pounding the east-facing window.

"We haven't been properly introduced," he said, filling his plate. They might forgo titles, his, and hers if she had one. "My name is—"

"There is no need," she said.

The sheer ferocity of the statement intrigued him. "Why?"

"When the storm ends, you will go your way, and I will go mine."

She ate then, in silence and quickly, like a schoolboy needing to finish before the dishes were removed. Or, since she took a second helping, perhaps like someone unsure of her next meal. But her table manners were otherwise impeccable.

Not having eaten since a quick breakfast that morning, Malcolm hurried through his meal as well before venturing again to begin a conversation.

"The ale is decent," he said. "A home brew?"

"As I pointed out, the Queen's Barque has a brewhouse."

A knock at the door brought a cheerful lad burdened by two straw-stuffed pallets. He was accompanied by a massive beast.

The dog cast Malcolm a curious gaze, and then went to the lady, tail wagging furiously.

"Hector." She knelt to receive slobbery kisses from the brindled mastiff, or, given the droopy ears and gloriously plumed tail, part mastiff. The dog stood a full yard at the shoulder, and when done kissing, grinned at her through its jowls.

"He hasn't forgot you my lady," the boy said.

She plucked a scrap from the tray and handed it to the dog.

"Was all well tonight, my lady? Mam was worried about..."

He froze, noticing Malcolm's interest.

"Everyone is well," she said. "Finishing up and returning home."

"Ah good, thank you, my lady. I'll be going then. Hector?"

"Hector is busy making my acquaintance," Malcolm said, for indeed the dog was sniffing his trousers and hands, and allowing his massive head to be fondled. "Ye're a fine fellow," he said. "Let him rest here a bit."

The boy looked a question at the lady and then shrugged. "He'll look after you then, my lady."

The dog was here to guard her from Malcolm? He laughed. Very well. But who would guard Malcolm from her?

When the door closed, she bustled about covering the food. *My lady*, the lad had called her, not once but four times. If she was a lady, what the devil was she doing out in trousers running cargo?

She hefted a bucket of water and went to the dark corner of the room.

In the light of the lamp, he'd seen that her eyes were blue, and her eyebrows were a dark shade of blond. A few freckles spotted the bridge of her nose, and delicate frown lines etched the space between her eyebrows. She was older, but not yet old.

She was far too young to be the lady he was seeking.

When she returned to the light, he saw that she'd finally shed the ugly cap, revealing shoulder length hair in a dark shade of blond, hair that shimmered in the lamplight, and made his fingers itch to explore.

A sudden flash of light streaked through the grimy windows. The storm gods had added lightning to their repertoire. The crack of thunder that followed evoked a whine and sent the massive dog pacing.

He beckoned, and the dog came and laid its head on his lap, adding slobber to the mud splattered on his only pair of trousers. He rubbed the loose skin and scratched behind a floppy ear.

"There'll be no sleeping soundly until the storm eases, I fear," she said. "Hector will make sure of it."

"Should I send him away, poor fellow?"

"No."

Whether she wished Hector to stay for her own safety or the dog's, he couldn't be sure, but her decisiveness pleased him. She wasn't a dithering sort of female. "As long as the building around us holds."

"It's withstood these storms for some three hundred years, they say. We must hope for the best." She went to a cabinet and returned with a bottle. "Brandy?"

"I've something better." He retrieved his flask from his bag. "Good whisky. The last of it. Share it with me?"

She nodded and accepted the glass he poured. "You are Scottish."

"Aye. Have ye ever seen a Scotsman before?" he joked.

"Where is your plaid, your... your kilt?"

"I've left it at home."

Her gaze narrowed on him. She clinked her glass to his, said "cheers," and took a tentative sip. "It's good."

"Aye. Are there many Scots here about?"

"I fear I don't know."

"But ye've kenned that I'm Scottish, and ye're from these parts. Ye would know were there others of my countrymen here."

She dipped her head. "No. I am not from these parts."

He heard it then—*non*, not *no*. She'd swallowed the n on the end of the word, the faint trace of an accent he'd noticed earlier and couldn't pin down. She was French. A French lady who'd recognized him as a Scotsman.

His hopes rose. *My lady*, the boy had called her. She wasn't from around here, she said, but neither was the lady he was seeking, the Comtesse de Fontenay. Mayhap this lady was her young sister, or a cousin, or some fellow émigré who might have once met the Earl of Menteith. She would know where another French lady was residing.

Yet she was a wary one, as wary as himself. She had no reason to trust him, and for his part, he might be risking having his throat cut—quite decisively.

More thunder crashed, and Hector raised his head again, howled and threw himself upon the lady. The dog's regard for her eased Malcolm's worries about her character.

More fool him.

He refilled both their glasses with the very last of the whisky and picked up the brandy bottle. "Come," he said. "I'll take one of those chairs by the fire. If ye like, stretch out on the sofa or one of those pallets."

She seated herself in the opposite chair, and they drank, silently. Hector settled himself on one of the pallets, making Malcolm laugh.

"I'm bluidy tired myself," he said.

"Go to sleep."

He studied her over the top of the tumbler. What had he been thinking, to share a chamber with this woman?

"You fear me, that I'll cut your throat in the middle of the night," she said. "I won't. Nor will I rob you."

Thunder boomed and Hector leapt up, looking between the both of them. She beckoned the beast, and he went to her for another head rub.

"Are ye giving me yer word as a lady?" he asked.

"Something like that."

"The boy called ye *my lady*."

She shrugged. "A mere courtesy."

The thoughtless arrogance of that tiny gesture spoke volumes. She might be an actress pretending to act the role of a noblewoman, but he didn't think so.

He would stay awake. A Scotsman could hold his liquor better than any mere lass, noble or not.

CHAPTER THREE

Most Assuredly Not His Mother

The handsome young Scotsman drank freely and deeply, refilling her glass, and she could see that he was willing himself to stay awake.

He did not appear to be a naïve man, or one of the countless fribbles that populated aristocratic circles. Perhaps he wasn't an aristocrat at all, but just some wealthy man of trade's sprout trained up to the air of command that was bred into the nobility.

No matter. Whatever his station in life, he was younger, and she was older. She had played this game more often, and, like any woman in a man's world, for higher stakes. What one lacked in muscle, one must make up for in cleverness, including the skill of holding one's liquor.

Besides, after spending yesterday morning diligently going through the Comte's dun letters, deciding who might be paid and who she might tell to go to the devil when she left for France, she'd had a very long afternoon nap, anticipating a call to help offload the lugger. The perilous weather meant all hands had been needed. She was not so very tired.

The Scotsman, however, was dead on his feet. She could almost feel sorry for him. He was far from home, and had been traveling for several days. His neckcloth was tired, his cuffs soiled, his coat wrinkled. His boots, well and carefully crafted, if not by Hoby then by some equally fashionable bootmaker in Edinburgh, had not been properly polished in the last few days.

He'd shaved though, probably very early that morning, because a delicious dark stubble had sprouted along his strong jaws.

Did he have a razor in his interesting valise? She wouldn't molest him, unless he thought to do the same to her. If it came to that, and she prayed that it wouldn't, she would use her own blade and not some unfamiliar shaving instrument.

"Is this one of your imports?" he asked, swirling the amber liquid. "It's very good."

His words stirred her out of her imaginings about handsome young men, and she realized she must manage the conversation else she'd slip into sleep, or perhaps something more inconvenient, without thinking.

The Comte had always succumbed to sleep when they'd conversed, no matter the topic.

She must soothe this fine-looking and very fatigued man the same way.

Outside, the thunderstorm had moved on, and the rain pounded in a comforting downpour. With the warm fire, and the heavy blankets, and the sleeping dog, it was quite cozy.

But what to talk about? Most certainly not the free trade. It would be far too diverting to put him to sleep, and besides she had no idea what he would do with the knowledge.

The countryside? She might slip and drop a hint about her home at Bloodmoor Hill.

She thought back to her time on the fringes of a London society that she'd found unbearably dull.

The weather.

"I am glad you are enjoying the brandy," she said. "But I daresay you are not liking this weather. It is quite the worst storm in many seasons, people are saying. Normally at this time of year the sea has quietened." A lie, of course, but how would he know?

He sipped his drink, eyeing her over the glass.

Oh. Given that it might remind him of her activities that evening and spark questions, the sea was an inappropriate topic, whether or not one was fudging a weather report. "Winters, however are generally mild."

He yawned, and she went on, discussing the number of rainstorms in March and going back to February, and then January, and making up the story as she went along, until his eyes drooped and the empty glass fell into his lap and lodged itself next to his fall.

Warmth uncurled in her. His trousers were tight in the usual fashion for gentlemen, outlining masculine endowments that sparked her interest far too much. Retrieving the fallen tumbler was out of the question.

She set down her own glass and fought the urge to join him in slumber.

***

Malcolm woke to a sense of unsettling awareness, eyes opening, the rest of him motionless. He was at yet another bluidy inn—ah yes, the road north had collapsed. He was with a fetching lady smuggler wearing trousers.

He'd fallen asleep in a chair and his neck ached like the devil, and... the chair opposite was empty, as was the sofa.

A steady gurgling snore came from the floor in front of him where the massive dog lay, and the rain still pounded. All else was silent.

The lamp on the mantel emitted a low light, as did the fire.

He carefully swiveled his head. A candle sat atop the dining table, next to his open travel bag. The woman bent close to the dim light, studying a paper.

In three silent strides he was on her. She squeaked, startled, while he gripped her around the waist and yanked her back into him.

This close she smelled of a floral soap and her hair tickled his nose. Her curves tickled other parts of him. He eased his grip on her, and she huffed out a quiet breath.

"I believe that's mine. What are ye doing, my lady?"

She turned her head to look up at him and shrugged. "Satisfying my curiosity, *my lord*."

Hot anger flared in him, warring with a begrudging acknowledgement that, if he'd lulled her to sleep first, and if she'd been carrying a bag to search, he'd have done the same.

And there was her distracting femininity, so close, so enticing, stirring a different kind of heat. He'd not had a woman since he broke with a Highland widow before traveling to London in February.

"Mayhap ye'd like me to satisfy aught else," he whispered.

She froze and then scoffed, relaxing into apparent indifference.

On the table next to where her hand lay was his sheathed razor. If she knew where his mind was traveling, she'd have every right to use it upon him.

He released her and backed away. "There's little of value there. If ye're looking for my weapons or my money, it's my person ye'll want to peruse."

She looked back at him again, her gaze traveling over him, her bowed lips curving up. "I am not in need of money," she said.

"A smuggler not in need of money. I don't think I believe ye." He fought the urge to grin back at her. "In any case, those are my things. It's rude to go through a gentleman's belongings unless ye're his valet. Or perhaps his wife. Kindly put everything back."

She left everything as it was and faced him. "Knowledge, my lord, is sometimes more valuable than money. *You* are no mere gentleman. *You* are an earl."

He had two documents in his bag, a letter addressed to him from an unfortunately anonymous sender, and the declaration of a witness to his birth.

She perched her hands on her shapely hips. "Who is threatening you?"

She'd been reading the letter.

He stared into glowing eyes, wondering about her interest. Wondering if he might trust her. "Why? Will ye help me find the sender?"

Her gaze traveled over him again, head to foot and then back up again. It had been assessing, not amorous. She frowned. "You are young. Perhaps...three and twenty?"

The skin on his neck quivered. "Precisely." He glanced at the bag and the few contents littering the table. The other document was less accessible, wrapped in an oilskin in an inner compartment. He felt certain she hadn't yet found it. "And ye know this how?"

"I know nothing."

She'd spoken too quickly. "Ye know that I am Scottish, that I am an earl, the Earl of

Menteith, and ye know my age. What else do ye know, my lady?"

"Nothing." She pushed past him, skirted the snoring dog, and stood by the warm hearth.

He followed and loomed over her, propping a hand on the carved wood of the mantel.

She seemed unsettled, perhaps because her search had been interrupted. She was a lady who liked to be in control.

His blood stirred. It was time to match wits with her.

"Shall I tell ye what *I* know?" He brushed a lock of hair from her cheek and her eyes flashed something between anger and fear.

Malcolm folded his arms over his chest. He'd given his promise as a gentleman that he wouldn't molest her. And he wouldn't.

However, if she were willing...

She lifted her chin. "You know nothing."

"I know ye are French."

A slim hand fluttered, dismissively. "There are many French émigrés in England."

"French and a lady. A noble lady? Or perhaps related to a noble lady... a *comtesse* perhaps."

Her gaze held steady.

"A *comtesse* who resides at Bloodmoor Hill Manor."

She blinked.

"Aye. Ye are a relative, or perhaps a friend of the Comtesse de Fontenay."

Her mouth opened and then closed, firming into a mulish line.

"What do you want with her?" she asked.

His heart lifted, excitement thrumming. *Finally*. After months of pondering since the letter arrived, after weeks of dreary searching, chasing about from Devon to Hastings, to Clackton-on-Sea, finally he'd found someone who knew the Comtesse—and he was sure this lady smuggler did know her.

"Will ye take me to her?" he asked.

A long thoughtful pause ensued. The bowed lips closed into an expression that was neither a pout nor a smile. The gaze revealed nothing—not curiosity, not fear, not suspicion.

A duchess who'd condescended to allow his introduction had worn the same haughty bland expression just before cornering him privately to express her interest in *something more*.

And he needed to stop thinking about the *something more*. His goal was in sight, and the goal was not swiving this lady, no matter how appealing.

"Why?" she asked, finally. "You must tell me why."

"Because..."

A reporter for a London rag sheltered next door in the inn. She might say she didn't need money, yet this tidbit of news he'd been protecting would bring someone a few coins.

He let out a breath. If need be, he had the scandal of a lady smuggler to barter. “She is my mother. My true mother.”

Her mouth dropped, her eyes widened, and softened. Her hand floated up and her palm cradled his cheek.

“It *is* you then. So handsome you are. Young, and yet not young. You have old eyes, Lord Menteith, and, I can see, a weary heart. And I confess, I am quite smitten.”

Smitten? She was smitten? They might have an entirely more pleasant evening together than what had transpired so far. But first he must secure a promise. “Will ye take me to her?”

She lifted her hand away and shook her head slowly. “Yes, but no, Lord Menteith.”

She’d moved close, her hands smoothing along his shoulders down to his elbows, her eyes full of a warm emotion that he couldn’t quite discern.

A lady smuggler entirely too close and too warm. His good sense ought to kick in, but his mind was too jumbled, his male parts on high alert.

“Yes, but no?” he repeated dumbly.

“Lord Menteith, *I* am the *Comtesse* de Fontenay. And I am most assuredly *not* your mother.”

“Ye’re...” His mind stuttered over the facts as she’d stated them. “My mother...” He rubbed at his forehead.

“I am *not* your mother.” She took him into her arms—’twas the only way to explain it—in an embrace that was maternal, but... oh what did he know about maternal affection? The woman he'd thought was his mother had died when he was a babe.

He became aware of the breasts crushed against him and the hands stroking his shoulders, and all of his male parts stirred. He swept a hand down the back of her sturdy wool coat, down to the shapely swell of her trousers.

And froze. She'd quite handily distracted him. He ought to be asking more questions.

"When did she die?" he asked, still holding her close. A handful of woman this fine was worth holding onto, even if she might be lying. "Or..." His cousin had divorced *his* wife. Perhaps Malcolm's mother still lived. "Did he put her aside? Where is the Comte? When did ye marry him?"

Another thought struck him. He had no certainty about who had sent the letter. This lady might be the anonymous correspondent.

CHAPTER FOUR

An Invitation

Marielle clutched him to her bosom, taking comfort from his great brawn and his masculine strength. For he was strong, this young man with the old eyes. In his long-limbed height, he put her in mind of her first lover, a lieutenant home recovering from wounds, a clumsy, ungainly fellow growing into his manhood, as unskilled as herself, but delightful and funny, able to distract her from thoughts of her country. When their affair was uncovered, her aunt had quietly married her off to the widowed Comte de Fontenay, an old roué with few teeth, a bald head that he draped with an old-fashioned wig, and dwindling abilities in the bedchamber.

Still, having learned from his past, the Comte had a sense of honor about his young wife's satisfaction, and from him, she'd learned things about men and about herself.

She had a sense of honor as well, and so, though Gaspar had kindly declared that she was free to take lovers, she'd been faithful to him until his death the previous autumn. And, been too picky about men since to enjoy her widowed state.

She felt certain the Comte would understand the heat stirring in her now.

Yet Menteith had many questions that first must be answered before any thoughts of an amorous congress. Marielle gathered her wits and stepped back from him.

First the unasked question she sensed was simmering within him. "I am not the letter-writer. That would *certainement* be another Scotsman, Giles Banquo."

His achingly handsome jaw dropped. "How—"

"We will come to that." Oh yes, he knew Banquo. His eyes had flared at the mention of a name that never failed to stir anger in her. "Your mother, who was the Comtesse de Fontenay before me, died in the Vendee, in the *populicide*, the revolutionaries' attempt to wipe out everything that was the old France."

Rage born of terrible memories and bitter despair flared in her, emotions that Gaspar had urged her to abandon lest they eat away her heart. She had mostly managed to constrain them within a firm cage of cynicism. But not entirely.

"The good and noble *citoyennes* turned out to be tyrannical and destructive beasts. It is an abomination that the son of this so-called revolution, Bonaparte, has been allowed to escape... to... to spread more death."

She took in a breath, squeezing her eyes against the emotion that overcame her whenever she thought about the chaos and tyranny and destruction of France. It had been five and twenty years since the Bastille fell, and still France was a cancer upon the world.

When she opened her eyes, she found him staring at her with something that looked like concern. He blinked, and his demeanor changed, and he again became the self-contained aristocrat gathering facts. "How exactly did she die? When? Where?"

"When and where, I don't know, but the Comte said she died by the guillotine." She shook her head. "So much death. It angers me so. They murdered the royals, they killed the nobles and priests, and then they devoured the bourgeoisie." Including her father, a doctor, and her mother, both executed after sending Marielle off to the country with an aunt. "And in the Vendee, they killed on a grander scale."

She'd been no more than a child when she sought refuge at her aunt's home in the Vendee. Before their narrow escape, she'd seen bloodshed that no child should ever witness.

She squeezed her eyes shut again on the visions. After a moment, she became aware of his hands, large and warm, cupping her shoulders. She lifted his hands away and took a breath, bringing herself into the present. "It was years before the Comte received proof of her death. They had come here, you see, quite prudently, after the Bastille fell, but she... she left him. She fell in love."

Menteith's gaze finally turned away from her as he looked into an unseen past.

"I had this story from the Comte himself."

He bit his lip. This news was a burden for him, but she must continue on.

"After your birth, she saw that there was no future with her lover. She returned to the Comte and soon after left to fight in the Royalist cause."

That Comtesse had left him, this handsome and noble son. How *could* she have done so?

"I might be the Comte's son."

His matter-of-fact tone belied a turmoil she sensed rising within him.

"No. He never fathered a child, not on your mother, not on me, nor on any lovers. Gaspar—the Comte—died last autumn. He knew of your birth, though I don't believe he sent that threatening letter to you either. However, before he died, he had a visit from Giles Banquo."

"I see." He walked to the table and poured another drink. Outside, the rain surged again, reminding them both of its power and its presence, the wind howling like the uneasy guilt eating away at her heart. It was Gaspar's guilt, yet he had left it to her as part of her meager inheritance.

"On his deathbed, he told me that he sold the story of your birth to Banquo for a price. He had little to leave me, you see. We had come here to this last lonely outpost because an old friend was engaged in the free trade. Gaspar had contacts in France and had done some business out of Devon and Kent. His heart was failing, and he was far too old for the endeavor, but he went out anyway and wore himself out. Then, last year, when he was ailing, he told me that Giles Banquo had advanced him money for the story and promised a grand sum if he could but find proof."

"And he never did?"

"Pay money? Or find proof?"

"Either. Both."

"The money advanced was spent on Gaspar's care." As for proof... was there proof? She had no idea. "And to my knowledge there is no proof. And it is no matter. I don't wish for his blood money."

"How did he come to know Banquo?"

"I don't know how Banquo came to visit us. But Banquo's wife was French, and Gaspar knew her family."

"I see."

He studied her for an uncomfortable moment while she straightened her spine and gazed directly back until the shame flooding her made her drop her eyes. What a dreadful inheritance Gaspar had left her.

"And so," he said, lifting her chin with two fingers, "you've taken up the Comte's smuggling." He reached for her, his eyes warm with unaccountable forgiveness and drew her into his arms. "Surely you cannot continue in the free trade?"

The kindness unsettled her. What sort of young man was this?

"I only help when needed. I am returning to France."

"What will you do there?"

"I will fight Bonaparte. I know, I cannot perhaps, take up arms like the infantry, but I can help in other ways. I can tend wounds, or pass information. And meanwhile, I will see about reclaiming my family home."

"My lady, it is twenty years gone."

"Yes. I know. I was a child of five when I left there. But I at least want to try if I may. Perhaps the new owner will rise for Bonaparte and be struck down with him, and then I may bring a lawsuit. It is worth the attempt. My parents were well off, but your mother, my lord, she was very rich. She was the sole heir of a large estate near La Roche-sur-Yon." Bile rose in her. "After they'd killed all the *Yonnais*, they changed the name of the town to Napoleon-sur-Yon."

Heart pounding, she leaned back and looked up at him. She had been alone for too many months now. She was a widow. She might take a lover if she wished. And she did wish. "Come with me to France."

His dark gaze burned down at her.

"At the manor, there are some things of your mother's that Gaspar kept. They mean little to me, and I haven't known what to do with them. I read the newspapers. The world is mobilizing against Bonaparte. We will not be alone in making our way to the Continent. Banquo..." She huffed out a breath remembering another reason she wished to disappear from Suffolk. "Is he following you?"

"No. Or I don't think so."

"He might show up anywhere, even in this terrible storm. We might find him in France, although what side he'll be fighting on is unclear."

His steady gaze sent goosebumps jumping along her back.

"We'll leave for Bloodmoor Hill Manor at first light," he said. "About the rest..." He traced a finger along her cheek, and under her neckcloth, and then went to work single-handed untying the knot.

The skilled touch sent shivers through her. The neckcloth fell away, as did the opening of the linen shirt.

She'd bound her breasts, as she always did. He dipped a finger under the cloth, watching her.

"Ye're certain we're not related?" he asked.

"I am certain. Your blood is much higher than mine, my lord."

"What is your name?"

"Marielle Plessiers. And you are Malcolm?"

"Yes. And for now, we're just a man and a woman."

She went up on her toes and their lips met. The storm picked that moment to rage harder, the wind howling again like the need boiling inside her.

He was virile, and strong, and a man in the prime of his mating years. Oh, how she wanted him.

CHAPTER FIVE

A Kiss Interrupted

Her soft lips tasted like brandy. Malcolm clasped her more closely, inhaling her scent of fresh sea air and soap whilst she trembled against him, as if the soul-baring tales of both his mother's suffering and her own had been true. His good sense told him to hold back trust. His heart said to comfort her. His base nature said she was his for the taking, and his base nature won out.

He pulled the tails of her shirt from her loose trousers and searched for the tie of the cloth binding her breasts, the need to see them, to touch them driving him mad. He found the knot, and unable to loosen it, ripped it, while his tongue dueled with hers and the cloth fell away.

Her loose coat slipped off easily, and he stepped back to look. The gaping shirt bared the tops of her breasts, a sight more alluring than all the bursting bosoms he'd seen at society events.

He inched the shirt hem up and slid his palm over the bare skin at her midriff to her waistband. "A dress on a lady is much more convenient than trousers."

She set a hand to his waist. "While a gentleman finds the trousers oh so very convenient."

Her blue gaze intent, she slid her palm down the front of his trousers and took in a sharp breath.

Malcolm watched her, reining in the urge to toss her down on the sofa and rip every stitch from her. He set his hand upon hers, and lifted it away. "Not yet," he said, easing a hand up to fondle her breast.

At his touch, her eyes closed and her head tilted back. "You are a patient lover, Malcolm Menteith?"

"Malcolm Comyn."

"What?"

"My surname is Comyn, Marielle."

He took her lips again and led her to the sofa, settling her back on the cushions, pushing her shirt up. He needed this. He needed her.

Voices outside made him look up. Hector jerked out of his slumber and lifted his nose in the air.

"Someone is coming," she said.

He muttered a curse. He'd failed to lock the outside door, and this door had no lock.

Marielle sprang to her feet and found her coats, while he went to the door and pressed his ear to the panel.

He recognized the innkeeper's voice and opened the door a crack. Lantern in hand, the innkeeper escorted a lady attired in a dark water-logged carriage gown. Another lady just as drenched followed behind carrying a valise.

"Begging your pardon, sir," said the innkeeper, spotting him.

Malcolm opened the door wider.

"We've more refugees from the storm. Husband and sons are helping fetch the fuel and the mattresses. We'll just get you upstairs then, madam, and we'll have you set up in a wink."

"Thank you," she said, her voice shaky, her relief obvious.

If they were only just arriving by carriage, they must have endured a terrible journey in this storm.

Hector pushed up next to him, Marielle following. She'd tucked her long hair into the damp cap, playing a boy again.

"Bring them in here to wait," Malcolm said. "I peeked in upstairs earlier. It's dry, but quite chilly. You may warm up at our hearth while your fire is made and your beds are set up."

The innkeeper nodded his thanks and hurried out, promising to send hot drinks.

***

Merde. What had she been thinking?

Marielle hustled about, fetching brandy for the two women while Malcolm took their wet wraps and set the warm blankets about their shoulders as if he were tending to his own mother or aunt.

Her eyes filled and she blinked, carrying the glasses over and silently handing them to the women.

They were soaked to the bone, their teeth chattering, and there were at least two feet of mud on the hems of their skirts. What once might have been lace on the older woman's gown now looked like spun mud. The ladies must have walked for a good part of their journey.

"What happened?' she asked, risking them recognizing that she was a woman.

She'd managed to fumble her coats closed and tie a loose knot on her neck cloth, but the cloth that had bound her breasts lay on the pallet. Fortunately, Hector had decided to retire again, and stretched himself over all but a wee bit of cloth. Sadly, she was well-enough endowed that her coats might not provide the right silhouette for the young man she was pretending to be.

She crossed her arms over her chest.

The maid—for Marielle was convinced the thin, more plainly dressed woman was a maid—sipped her drink and choked.

"It's brandy," Malcolm said, coming to stand next to Marielle. "A fine one, for those who are used to the taste. Sip it. It will help to warm you."

The older lady unclenched her chattering teeth long enough for a sip. "We thank you. It's very good."

"What happened?" Marielle asked again. She really needed to know the state of the roads. While the storm still raged, they would wait; but at the first sign of the weather easing, they must be off. She would like to depart for France before Banquo decided to pay a call. "Were you coming from Lowestoft?"

The road from Lowestoft had collapsed, but despite what Malcolm had said about the marshland, they might have made their way around on foot.

"No, we were traveling north on the coast road," the maid said, launching into a tale of woe.

Marielle stepped into the shadows, listening.

Bloodmoor Hill Manor stood to the south and west of Lowestoft. The road was impassible, but in normal times, she could find her way through the marshes and fields. They might also take the westerly road and pick their way north. However, if that road was impassible, if the path through the marshes was flooded, she still didn't wish to remain in Fenwick on Sea. She didn't wish to remain in England at all. As soon as the downpour eased, she must make the attempt to leave.

And Malcolm would be with her. Though he didn't know the land hereabouts, she would not be alone. That knowledge made her braver.

The ladies had finished their tale and had begun asking questions that Malcolm was amiably deflecting, whilst sounding like a Mayfair fribble, hiding most of the clipped and inflected Scottishness of his speech. Which accent was true? Could she trust him?

From her chair in the dark corner of the room, she watched and listened. Malcolm was hiding from the scandal sheet reporter as was she. Like herself, he didn't have a good face for dissembling, and he'd taken himself off to the shadows as well. Though no lady with blood in her veins would forget that handsome profile.

Malcolm Comyn, the handsome young Earl of Menteith—the letter she'd perused in his bag had claimed to have proof that he was not the true earl. And she felt certain she'd seen that handwriting before in a letter Banquo had sent her mere weeks ago.

Malcolm's father ought not to have put him through this. If one could not trust one's own father...

She sighed. Life was precarious and there were always battles to be fought over property and money. And trust... *pah*. Trust was a rare commodity.

She'd trusted the Comte, though he wasn't entirely a good man, and rarely a law-abiding one. But what were men's laws? They changed with the government or one's social standing. Good character was something more basic.

Having watched Malcolm comfort Hector and tend to the ladies, she decided he was altogether a good man. It was perhaps too impulsive, but she'd also decided she must find a way to convince him to come with her to France. He hadn't actually agreed to go any farther than Bloodmoor Hill.

***

Malcolm escorted the ladies up the stairs and returned to find the lamp doused and the fire low. As he entered, Marielle stepped out of the shadows. She'd taken the cap off and was brushing her hair—with his brush.

He laughed. "Searching again?"

"Only for this. And thank you for the use of it."

He shoveled more coal into the fire. "What do ye think? Can we find our way to Bloodmoor Hill tomorrow?"

Outside the storm picked that moment to blast rain at the window.

"Not if this downpour continues. But if it slows in the morning, we may try, I think." She came to stand next to him. "Tonight, we must sleep."

"How do I know ye won't leave without me? This fellow here," he pointed at Hector who was again fast asleep, "won't warn me."

"Do you mean to bind me to you?" she asked in a teasing tone.

His male parts stirred and he touched her shoulders. "Would ye like that? I've better means of persuasion than that."

She laughed. "No, my dear young Earl of Menteith. We will sleep tonight. However, I shall make sure you accompany me when I leave, because at Bloodmoor Hill Manor, there is a very comfortable bed."

She moved behind him, helping him out of his coat, and tugging his hand to join her on the remaining pallet. "We shall not disturb Hector. If there are fleas, they will visit his bed and not ours."

Malcolm laughed, allowing himself to be led. She was unaccountably trusting to bed down with a lusty young man. "Where is yer blade, madame Comtesse?"

"In my boot, which I will leave on in case there are unwelcome arrivals this night."

Something—or someone—worried her. Perhaps Banquo.

She stretched next to him and rolled on her side, facing the fire, her delectable bottom flush against him.

How could he possibly sleep? This was torture.

Nevertheless, he shut his eyes and tried.

"Malcolm," she said softly "tell me how you know Giles Banquo."

"That is a topic sure to squash any romance. He's a distant cousin."

"And he would inherit if you are illegitimate?"

"There is another cousin before him, Finnley Macbeth." He shifted the scratchy blanket they were using as a pillow. "Shall I tell ye the tale, Comtesse?"

Was there a risk trusting her? He wasn't sure that he gave a damn, not anymore.

"Will it put me to sleep?"

He chuckled. "I'm weary to death of it, Comtesse, so perhaps it will."

She rolled over to face him, a hand tucked under her head. Close enough to kiss.

"Tell it," she said.

Glad for the unexpected intimacy, he dropped a kiss on her forehead and draped an arm over her. "Once upon a time, there was a Scottish lord, the Thane of Menteith, who had three wives. He put the first one aside, and then the second as well, and then took a third. Each wife bore him at least one son, but 'twas the son of the second marriage, his mother having been his favorite, and him having regretted divorcing her, who the title passed down to." He touched a finger to her cheek. "Your eyes are still open."

"I am being polite." She smiled and shifted under him with one of her Gallic shrugs. "And I am usually awake at this time. When I'm needed to help, it is usually at midnight."

"The Comtesse of Midnight."

She smiled. "If you wish. Please go on."

"There were feuds through the centuries over the inheritance, but my ancestors held on through the generations up to my father, Duncan Comyn."

"And you."

"If I'm a bastard, the title goes to my cousin, Finnley Macbeth."

"Is he working with Banquo?"

"No. Macbeth feuded with my father over the title twenty years past, and almost killed him in a duel. A few weeks ago, in London, Macbeth was attacked by footpads. I believe Banquo was behind that attack."

"This Macbeth is alive?"

"Yes. His man and I arrived in time."

"He is alive because of you. That was very noble."

Unease threaded through him. Was Macbeth still alive? His injuries had not been life threatening, but it was possible another attempt had been made. He ought to have written to his aunt, Lady Fiona, except that he'd had no fixed address to receive a reply.

"He might have prevailed with just the help of his servant. Macbeth is a soldier. He spent the last twenty years fighting the French. The years have otherwise mellowed him—he told me the title is mine, and he's pledged me his sword."

"I see. He is noble, as well. Will he return to fight Bonaparte?"

"I don't know. He was recovering from a wound he received at Toulouse. And I left London before the news of Bonaparte's escape arrived."

"So, Banquo was in London as well?"

"Yes. That letter ye lifted out of my bag was mailed from there, and I'd gone to investigate. Macbeth was there on half pay, seeking employment. As it happened, Greer and Lucie, his wife—that is, his former wife—and his daughter had joined me in London."

She went very still.

"We were all guests of my great aunt, Lady Fiona Carlin." He touched her nose. "Ye must not be jealous. For certain, Greer has been reunited with Finnley, and Lucie is much like a sister to me. She's much like ye in that she occasionally dons trousers. Do not worry, she wouldn't have me as a spouse, and the feeling is mutual."

"I am, of course, not jealous."

He chuckled "Of course. But if ye were, I should be very flattered."

"If I flatter you, I fear that your head will swell so much you will not allow me any sleep tonight."

He laughed out loud, rousing Hector, who grumbled and set his chin on Malcolm's hip.

"The chaperon will keep me in line."

She raised up on her elbow and fondled the dog's head. "He is a good boy. But what is this about your cousin having a former wife?"

"He divorced Greer many years ago, believing she'd been unfaithful."

"Was she?"

"She was caught speaking with my father, and then later was discovered to be with child."

"The girl... Lucie?"

"Yes. And she is certainly Macbeth's. Ye've only to see them together to know it. Greer denied any affair and I believe her."

"This was the reason for the duel?"

How perceptive she was. "Yes."

"And he divorced her. I take back what I said about your cousin being noble. Perhaps he's as big a villain as Banquo."

"Perhaps, but I doubt it. In any case, he's acknowledged Lucie as his."

"Malcolm, do you suppose Banquo is still in London?"

"I don't know."

She bit her lip.

"What is it, Marielle?"

CHAPTER SIX

Bloodmoor Hill

"A letter came from him two weeks ago. He rambled on about many things. He wanted what papers Gaspar held about your mother and your birth. I can only think that Gaspar had baited him. Unbelievably, he also wrote of desiring all of the trade in these parts, which is *certainement*, not mine to give. Nor was it Gaspar's. There are many players between here and Yarmouth."

She shivered and he drew her closer. "Did he threaten ye, Marielle?"

"He will give testimony against me, so he says. He claims to have influence with the Riding Officer, and undoubtedly, he does, or rather, his coins do. We all pay the man to feign blindness, but Banquo has deeper pockets than I. If it were merely a matter of being deported to France, I would not worry, but I might be transported to the end of the earth. It is another reason I want to leave England."

"Ye're French nobility."

"Only by marriage. And... there is the threat of him reporting me as a spy. I am not a spy. That is, I would never spy for France as it has been for the last five and twenty years."

Spying from bluidy Bloodmoor Hill Manor, a place so isolated and remote he hadn't been able to find it? Possibly, but her denunciation of Bonaparte had seemed genuine to him.

He remembered what she'd said about the Comte having contacts in France. "Was the Comte a spy?"

She sighed. "Not as I am aware."

"Why didn't ye leave right after the Comte's death? Bonaparte was defeated months ago."

"There was the matter of settling Gaspar's debts, selling things as I am able. I needed money for the journey, as well. I did ponder what I might give Banquo. He has plagued me with requests for more than I can give." She bit her lip. "Or will give. I want to be gone before he shows up in Suffolk."

"Has he...has he harmed ye in other ways? If he's laid a hand on ye—"

"I would put out his eyes first." She grimaced. "And other friends would take note. I am not entirely undefended. The people near Fenwick on Sea, they have been kind to both me and to Gaspar while he lived, and I return the kindness when they need extra hands. You would not have discovered me if we'd gone out at our regular time. In fact, I could not imagine there would be any travelers after the coast road washed out and the westerly road was flooded. I am astonished that more have arrived. I do hope Banquo is not among them. I fear I will have to do him harm."

"Ye will leave that task to me."

She sighed and her eyes fluttered shut, a lock of hair falling across her cheek. She looked young and vulnerable and the urge to protect her was overwhelming, even more powerful than the desire to make love to her.

One long-lashed eye opened. "You are watching me," she said.

"Tomorrow, we'll travel to Bloodmoor Hill. Then we'll gather your things and go north to Yarmouth." With troops mobilizing, the inns there might be crowded. "We'll stop first at Lowestoft. I'll need to write to my factor and send an express to my aunt and find out what has happened to Macbeth and Banquo. We'll need things—clothing, supplies. Then, we'll travel to France together." He touched his lips to hers. "Sleep now."

She set her hand atop his and studied him, eyes growing shiny. "Thank you," she whispered.

He watched as her eyes drifted closed. On one side, the fire cast a steady heat their way and on the other, the dog lay sharing his warmth.

The crackling of the fire and the dog's snoring and Marielle's quiet breathing soothed him. Upstairs, the rustling and footsteps had died, the late arrivals having settled in after a day of exhaustion.

He should do the same, but his mind was a jumble. Much as he'd have liked to have found his mother and know that undiscovered side of himself, he wasn't a bit disappointed with the comtesse he *had* found.

Whatever the Comte had kept of his mother's, he wanted to see it. He wanted to understand why she'd left him, her son, in the untenable position of fighting for a title that wasn't his.

And why had his father put forth the lie? That, perhaps, was the bigger question, for Father had certainly felt guilt over the deception and thus had been more than generous in helping Greer and Lucie. He only wished his father had summoned the courage to tell him the truth before he died, instead of wasting his last words relating a witch's prophecy that Macbeth and Banquo's son would each hold the title.

That was one story he'd not shared with Marielle this night. Astonishing, how much he'd confided in her, this Comtesse de Fontenay.

The question was, when the weather settled, when the skies cleared and they were able to set out for her manor, would she lead him a merry chase? Probably, he decided, at least until their common enemy, Giles Banquo, was disposed of, one way or another.

***

Clouds layered the horizon in shades of gray with occasional glimpses of blue sky. Yet, as they left Fenwick on Sea and rode west, the rain still fell, steady, silent, and soft, as if they were riding into a lifting mist.

Marielle reached the edge of the navigable road and reined up, deciding the best approach. Ahead, the path dipped into a newly created lake. To either side ran marshland, here and there bordering on fields that had recently been cultivated. Some farmer generations ago had labored to drain those fields, and God had laughed, turning them back into mire.

Malcolm reined up next to her. "Any crops planted will be ruined."

She glanced over at him and found him frowning with real concern. "You farm, my lord? Oh, of course you do." This serious young man wouldn't be one of those lords who merely swanned about London—or perhaps Edinburgh—having new coats made, visiting his clubs and dueling studios.

"I have a home farm and tenants. So yes, I know about this sort of loss and the lean times it might bring." He shook his head. "I *had* a home farm and tenants is more appropriate, I suppose."

He was still thinking about Banquo's threat.

"Why don't you fight for the title?" Malcolm hadn't impressed her as soft or weak. "You are still the Earl of Menteith. Will you give it all up so easily? Banquo may bring suit, but you may tie him up for years in court. Or he may die before he can make the claim." Yes, that would be preferable. "And then no one will know the truth of your maternity."

"*I* will know the truth." There was steel in his voice, and a good bit of impatience. "Now, are we able to travel farther, or must we turn back to the Queen's Barque and wait for the weather and roads to clear?"

Returning to the inn was in neither of their best interests. They'd risen early, awakened by Brewster's daughter bringing breakfast, and then Malcolm had saddled both their horses, since the ostlers were busy seeing to yet another carriage that had straggled in.

She wiped moisture from her face. "Look at those patches of blue sky. I do believe the storm is weaker to the west. Let us try to find our way through. If need be, there are some humble cottagers around who may allow us to sleep with their cow."

"Instead of their dog? Lead the way."

He laughed, sending shivery warmth through her, as if she was a lighthearted young girl again. Her comfortable bed could not come too soon.

The rain did, indeed, diminish as they navigated through the marshes, seeking higher ground, zig-zagging through the Suffolk countryside. They paused in a circle of stones laid out on high ground and ate the luncheon Mrs. Brewster had packed for them.

It was late afternoon when they reached the gently sloped wooded ground near

Bloodmoor Hill Manor. They hadn't conversed much the last part of the journey. Marielle had silently worried over her horse, who deserved better treatment, and Malcolm, on his steady gelding, had seemed immersed in his own thoughts.

Still, at every path that might prove precarious, he'd insisted on going first. She'd allowed it, only because the trust he'd placed in her ought to be reciprocated. And for the sake of her horse, of course.

"How much farther?" he asked, moving up alongside her.

She reined up and patted her mount. To the left, a narrow footpath reached deep into the wood, the dense foliage around it beaten down by the rain, so that they could see a cottage beyond with its rude clearing and a boy throwing feed to a smattering of chickens.

"Not far," she said. "Those are my neighbors."

Spotting them, the boy waved and scampered through the brush toward them.

"My lady," he said, short of breath. "Da feared you were lost."

"He is safely home?"

"Aye."

"And so am I. Is all well here?"

His gaze slid to Malcolm.

"You may speak freely, Hal," she said.

"I saw someun in the woods, not more'n an hour ago."

Dread slithered through her.

Hal glanced up the path that led to the manor. "Mam said not to wake Da yet. He was up all night saving the roof."

"What did the someun look like?" Malcolm asked.

"'Twas a man. A witchy sort. Gave me goosebumps. Had hair growing back from here." He smacked his forehead. "And a streak, like the devil's touch."

Her pulse quickened, and she drew in a breath, trying to swallow her fear, reminding herself she must be brave. Banquo was here for one final attempt to bully her. And it would be final. She would not run, nor would she cower. She had found the rightful owner of the letters Gaspar had been holding, and thanks be to God, this stalwart and brave young man had come with her.

She prayed he could fight as well as he could kiss.

Malcolm fished in a pocket and produced a coin, holding it up. "Does your da have any dry powder, Hal?"

Hal frowned up at her, seeking guidance.

"Malcolm, a poor man with a gun and powder might bring down some lord's precious game to keep his family from starving," she whispered. "A capital offense."

He frowned, and nodded.

"This is Lord Menteith, Hal," she said. "We may trust him. But Malcolm, I do not think we should trouble Hal's father."

Nor did she wish to involve the poor man in what most certainly would be an ugly confrontation. Perhaps a taking of life. "Was it only the one man?" she asked. "Was there anyone else with him?"

"Not as I saw. And I followed him. He smashed out yer window. Knocked all the glass out." His eyes had gone round. Housebreaking was another serious offense.

"Very well. I'm glad he didn't disturb your family." She turned to Malcolm. "Do give him the coin, please."

"Hal," Malcolm called. "Catch it." He leaned down and let the coin drop into the boy's outstretched hand. "If the lady raises the alarm, ye must fetch your da. Understood?"

Hal eyed the coin and solemnly nodded.

"Go home now, sweetling," Marielle said. "And do not worry. I will be fine. Lord Menteith is with me."

Malcolm frowned, watching Hal scurry home.

"Hal's father was out with me yesterday. Banquo is fortunate he didn't harass them, for I would certainly have had to address *that* with him as well."

"Aye." Malcolm grimaced. "He has much to answer for. Come, Comtesse." He beckoned her, turned his mount off the path into a quiet clearing, and dismounted. "Even alone, Banquo is dangerous. Let us make a plan."

CHAPTER SEVEN

Banquo's Visit

"If ye won't wait with your neighbors," Malcolm said, "I insist I go in first."

The blasted woman had been quietly arguing with him since they dismounted in the small clearing. She refused to stay behind. She insisted she must confront Banquo.

Now, her mouth primmed into a hard line, and he sensed her ire under all that controlled detachment.

He reached for her, and she shrugged out of his grasp.

"Marielle, he's a dangerous enemy, and it's me he's after."

"And I would let you take all the risk? It's my home, Malcolm, and I insist I must go with you to face Banquo and I must confront him first."

The brush rustled, and he reached for his pistol. The man who approached through the trees had a care-worn face under a beat-up cap.

"Wythe," Marielle said. "I'm sorry Hal woke you."

"Twyla thought you might need my help. And Hal mentioned you asked about powder."

This neighbor of Marielle's might talk some sense into her where he himself was failing.

"I'd be much obliged for the powder," Malcolm said. "And if ye've a barn, mayhap the horses can rest there."

***

Bloodmoor Hill Manor proved to be a manor house as ancient as Malcolm's own country home, but smaller and far more decrepit. Marielle had informed him that her only servant was Hal's mother, Twyla, who came in a few times a week to cook, clean and tend to the laundry.

And it appeared there was little inside to clean. As dusk fell and they reconnoitered around peering through windows, he saw that most of the public rooms were sparsely furnished.

A small parlor at the back of the house held a table, benches, and near the fireplace, two overstuffed wingchairs. In one of them sat Banquo. He'd made himself a crackling fire and seemed to be staring into it. His hands rested upon his lap, and whether or not he had a pistol, Malcolm couldn't be sure.

At the back entrance, Malcolm set a hand to Marielle's arm. He must make one last attempt to make her see sense. "I'll go first."

Her eyes glittered with determination and more courage than many men had. "No."

A formidable woman was the Comtesse. He dropped a kiss on her lips. "I'm right behind you, then."

She used her key on the kitchen door, and they went through, meeting the smell of burnt toast. The coals in the hearth glowed, and a tea kettle rested on a central worktable. He set his hand to it—still warm.

He stayed on her heels as they tiptoed into a corridor. Age-old damp wood and mildewed wall coverings gave off a familiar scent, and the dust motes floating in the last glimmer of twilight attested to the shortage of both servants and the money for upkeep—for the last century probably. Marielle stopped at a door, straightened her shoulders and stepped into that back parlor.

"Banquo," she said. "What a surprise."

Banquo sat in a puddle of lamplight with his chair angled toward the fire.

"Marielle." He cleared his throat loudly. "Close the door."

"I will close it as you are leaving," she said coolly. "I feel no obligation to offer you hospitality. Do not let me detain you. Be on your way."

Banquo made a grumbling noise low in his throat and wheezed out a rattling cough. "Not leaving," he said.

Marielle took another step. “You are ill?” She laced the words with sarcasm. “You are bringing illness into my home?”

“Come. Sit, Marielle.”

Malcolm heard the pain in the raspy wheezing that followed, as if the man was barely holding himself together.

She moved closer and turned to confront the unwelcome visitor. Heart pounding, Malcolm stepped through the doorway.

“I think not, Banquo,” Marielle said.

“You haven’t always been such a bitch. You used to enjoy my company.”

Color rushed to her cheeks. “The Comte and I may have *suffered* your company,” she said. “We never enjoyed it.”

“Ah, Marielle. So beautiful. I had hoped—”

“Banquo.” She shifted a step nearer to Malcolm. “You are holding a pistol. In my home, you are holding a pistol. Why? Is it your plan, then, to shoot me?”

“Have you come alone?” He wheezed out the words. “I saw that lad watching.”

“Have you come alone?” she asked.

“She’s not alone, Father.”

The voice came from Malcolm’s left. He turned in time to catch an upraised arm. Steel glimmered in the hand attached to a lad of no more than twelve or thirteen. With a quick tug, he wrenched the lad’s hand and squeezed until the blade dropped.

In London, Banquo had told him he had two sons. This was one of them, too young and skinny for this task.

"It's all right, Giles," Banquo said.

Banquo leaned past the wing of the chair so that Malcolm could see the side of his face. Banquo's attention however, was on Marielle, and he'd aimed his pistol at her.

The blasted woman ought to have listened to him.

Malcolm latched the lad closer and drew his own weapon. "Ye don't want to do that, Banquo."

"Your powder's wet. Mine isn't."

"Shall ye risk it?" Malcolm asked, managing to keep his voice calm.

"Father," the boy said breathlessly.

Malcolm pressed the cold steel to the lad's temple. "Is this twig to be the next Earl of Menteith when ye unveil the scandal ye've concocted?"

"My second son." He huffed. "Has an elder brother."

Banquo appeared to be struggling for breath.

"You truly are ill," Marielle said. "Lower the pistol and I will send for the apothecary. Come, tell me what is wrong with you."

Malcolm shared a long steadying look with her. If she offered kindness, he could draw Banquo's ire his way. They hadn't got further than arguing over who would go first, but this seemed a good plan. Besides, Banquo wouldn't shoot her until he had whatever proof she was holding. He hoped.

"Lower your pistol, Banquo. Unless ye mean for this second twig of yours to be sacrificed when ye shoot the Comtesse."

She glanced at him, chin raised in haughty indignation. "Really, my lord? You mean to shoot a child?"

"If Banquo fires that weapon at ye? Aye, and straight through the lad's bluidy big ear."

The boy squirmed, and Malcolm tightened his grip, fighting back a surge of anger that was making this more than a role he was improvising.

"You'll swing if you kill me," the boy cried.

"Ye're a blasted little beggar who attacked me with a blade. I'll have shot ye in self-defense."

Marielle sent him a meaningful look, dipped her head, and he followed her gaze back to Banquo. The villain's hand trembled around the pistol, and his face glowed pale in the light.

"Let us cut to the chase," Marielle said. "Why are you here, Banquo?"

A laugh rattled out of him. "Knew you'd search, Menteith. Only had to set you on the trail. Find everything I needed. Knew you'd end up here, and she'd give you the proof. Ought to have waited another day." A great hacking cough shook him. "Damned storm."

Malcolm shuffled closer, holding the boy as a shield. "Is your brother here also, lad?"

"Father..." The boy trembled.

"Your brother," Malcolm said, pressing the barrel harder. "Where is—"

"He's in London."

"Ah. Did he go to London to finish the task of killing Lord Macbeth?"

"What?" The lad's shocked gaze slid his way.

"Lord Macbeth. He's the cousin who stands between me and your bluidy father for the title."

"Macbeth's dead," Banquo mumbled.

His breath caught. He ought to have written to Lady Fiona. He ought to have asked for news on Macbeth.

"*Certainement*, you are bluffing, Banquo," Marielle said, her nonchalant tone steadying him.

"Greer's dead too."

Pain ratcheted through him. Marielle turned a determined look his way, and then she rolled her eyes, again bringing him back to his senses.

Aye. She was right. Banquo might well be bluffing. In fact, he likely was. Lady Fiona would have scoured all of England to carry that news to him. Or he would have seen it in a newspaper. The murders of the scandalous Lord and Lady Macbeth would have earned a column between the Corn Riots and Bonaparte's escape.

He rallied his wits. "Is this your father, young sprig? A bluidy devil who goes about killing innocent ladies?"

"'S'enough." Banquo spluttered, his mouth contorting. He planted his feet and raised the pistol in both hands.

Malcolm caught Marielle's eye, and gave a jerk of his head, praying she'd know to duck. Then he shoved the boy hard, knocking him into his father.

A shot rang out. Yellowed stuffing burst from the worn damask upholstery of the opposite chair. The lad screamed and hit the floor, his father toppling upon him.

CHAPTER EIGHT

A Proposal

Banquo lay still and unmoving.

"You shot him," the boy cried.

Hand trembling, Malcolm raised Marielle from the floor where she'd dropped. No blood stained her clothing, the chair, or either of the tumbled bodies.

"Lord Menteith did not fire his weapon," Marielle said, her coolness again settling his nerves. "But your father has ruined my chair." She slipped an arm around Malcolm's waist. "You wouldn't really have killed that child?"

Heart pounding, he glanced at her, the full weight of the stakes they'd been playing hitting him.

He swallowed a rising bile. Except for his bad blood, the lad was likely an innocent. Likewise, except for her smuggling, so was Marielle. He hoped.

Oh, damn, he wanted the chance to find out.

"Get off me, Father," the boy cried, shoving at the dead weight atop him.

The shiver that went through her belied her calm demeanor, and he dropped a kiss on her forehead. "I'll buy ye a new chair from Chippendales. Two new chairs, since the other one ought to be shot as well. Have ye a rope?"

"Are we hanging the boy?" she asked. "I must object."

Shocked eyes looked up at them. "I didn't do anything."

"Is your father dead?" Marielle asked. "Poke him, if you please."

He complied, and Banquo groaned.

"Search him," Malcolm said.

The boy retrieved another pistol and three daggers, and then submitted to his own pat down by Marielle.

"How long has your father been ill?" she asked.

"He has a... a festering wound. I don't know how long he's had it. He fetched me from school in Norwich a few days ago and said we were going to Yarmouth. But we stayed at an inn near my school and an apothecary came and treated him until his fever abated. He said we must come here first before Yarmouth and settle some business." He frowned, his eyes shining with tears he was valiantly fighting. "Do you know whether my brother is safe, sir? Father summoned him from school four weeks ago."

Malcolm and Marielle shared a look.

"Summoned him?"

"He sent orders and money for him to travel to London and join him there."

"And then he came to your school, wounded, pulled you out, and your brother is nowhere to be found?" The boy was right to be worried. If there'd been a fight that took both Malcolm and, God forbid, Greer, Banquo's elder son might have been killed as well.

Unless it was all part of Banquo's bluff.

"I don't know. I left London three weeks ago myself," Malcolm said. He stowed his weapon. "Come, help me get your father to a bed. I know the Comtesse has at least one bed here."

"That villain is not occupying my bed," she said. "Come along this way."

***

Malcolm stood in the doorway of the humble room off the kitchen where he and the boy had settled Banquo. Once a servant's bedchamber with a narrow bed that was no more than a cot, the room depended on the warmth of the cookfire seeping in through the doorway. It was likely freezing in winter.

However now, with three bodies crammed into the small space on this April evening and a fire in the kitchen hearth, only the man on the bed was shivering, delirious with fever.

He wished for the man to die, the sooner the better, and then felt a surge of guilt when he thought of the lad.

Not long after they'd shuffled Banquo into bed, Wythe and two of the other near neighbors had appeared, having heard the gunshot. With the villain already secure, Marielle had sent them to fetch hot meals from Wythe's wife, Twyla. Now the neighbors sat at the kitchen table, drinking ale and waiting to take turns guarding Banquo.

Malcolm had watched as Marielle tended Banquo's nasty wound, applying the salve provided by the apothecary in Norwich, and done what she could to help curb the fever. Though for the life of him, Malcolm couldn't see the point of trying to save the man. Except for the lad's sake, perhaps.

All this over a title, and the money and power that went with it. No one ever thought of the burdens. He had a good factor and land steward, but he couldn't go haring off to France forever. For two cents he'd hand everything over to... to whom? Macbeth, if he lived, didn't want it. This fatherless lad wasn't prepared for the task. Likely as not, his elder brother wasn't either. And if either of them proved to be chips off of Banquo's block, he'd skewer them himself. The people at home in Menteith deserved better.

Marielle rose, signaling one of her men to take her place next to the bed. "If he speaks, call us. Come with me, Malcolm."

Lantern in hand she led him through the corridor into the main hall, and then up two flights of creaky stairs to a large chamber.

A rare bit of moonlight filtered in through the uncovered windows. The room was completely devoid of furniture.

"No comfortable bed here," he said. "Not that there'll be any sleeping tonight."

She grimaced. "Such inconvenient visitors. But I don't wish to delay this task." She settled the lantern she'd carried on the mantel and pressed a bit of nearby paneling. A section of panel swung inward and she reached in. "This room was the Comte's bedchamber. He had a fine suite of furniture that was his property. The landlord accepted it for the last rent."

He joined her and peered into the small space. "No stacks of gold coins?"

She withdrew something small and closed the panel. "This is, perhaps, more valuable than gold to you. Come along."

He followed her through a different door into a connected private parlor where she settled the lamp and the items she'd withdrawn from safekeeping onto the table. "There is also a box with a few small items—a handkerchief, paste jewelry, a prayer book—that I must find for you, but these, the Comte kept hidden." She pulled out a chair. "Be seated. I will return directly."

She left through yet another door, this one on the opposite wall, and he looked around. This room had three doors, to the Comte's bedchamber, the corridor, and what must be her bedchamber. Besides the table and chair placed near the window, only a slipper chair and foot stool sat near the unlit hearth.

The shawl thrown over the back of the chair was definitely feminine. This sparsely furnished chamber was her sitting room.

’Twas true he was still a wealthy earl. She deserved so much better, and if he held onto the title, he could provide it for her.

He picked up the items she’d dropped: two letters, both seals still intact. He held the thicker one up to the light and his breath caught. The hand was his father’s, addressed to the Comtesse de Fontenay.

Yet Marielle hadn’t opened it?

The second was thinner, both the paper and handwriting equally delicate. *To my son, Malcolm.*

Heart pounding, he held it up to the light, and then to his nose catching the faint scent of a woman’s perfume. His mother’s perfume?

As he weighed each letter, deciding which tugged harder at his heart, he heard a pounding on the stairs.

“My lady,” a man called.

Marielle poked her head through her bedchamber door. “See what’s afoot, Malcolm.”

He went to the door that led to the corridor.

Wythe stood, hat in hand. “He’s come around, sir. Asking for ye.”

“I’ll be right down.”

He tucked the letters into his coat. “Banquo is awake,” he called.

“Help me first.”

She appeared in her doorway and his breath caught again. She'd shed her trousers and coats and donned a woman's dress, one that showed all of her womanly curves to full advantage.

"Do not gawk, Malcolm. Fasten this dress for me and quickly." She turned and lifted her hair away. "I assume you have some experience with ladies' gowns?"

"Not much, and ever clumsy."

"I doubt that."

"How do ye manage this without a maid?"

"I haven't worn this gown since before my maid left. But I knew you were here and would see to it for me."

He fastened the last hook, and let his hands slide down to her bottom, memorizing the shape of her. She turned in his arms and looked up at him. "There will be time, later. Let us see what Banquo has to say on his deathbed."

"He is dying then?"

"I doubt he will last the night." She bit her lip. "I had much experience with anticipating death while tending to Gaspar those last months."

"Ye were a good wife," he said. "Too young to have been—"

"You've never asked, but I am nine and twenty, not a young woman at all. And Gaspar wasn't unkind." She shrugged. "Come. I feel very sad for the boy. He is alone and adrift, I fear."

He followed her down the corridor and stairs, thinking about her heartfelt request that he come with her to France. With the Comte dead, Marielle was alone and perhaps adrift as well. But not any longer, if she would have him.

He caught up with her and ushered her into the sick room.

Banquo's eyelids fluttered. "Menteith," he whispered.

***

"Giles." Marielle caught the eye of the boy seated beside the bed and nodded to him. Tears hid behind the boy's long dark eyelashes, valiantly held back. Perhaps, with the right hand to guide him, he'd grow into a better man than his father.

A father who reappeared at the last and would be wrenched from him... She opened her mouth thinking to order him from the sick room, and decided against it. He was old enough to face this death.

"I am here, Banquo." Malcolm's harsh tone shattered the silence. "What is it ye wish to say?"

Malcolm's jaw had frozen as hard as steel. It was a wonder to her that he could speak at all.

"You're a bastard."

"And ye're dying. What scheme do ye have unfurling upon your death? Is there a solicitor somewhere who'll be unleashing a story to the scandal sheets?"

The words had been blunt and direct, and rather harsh for the boy's ears, but at least Malcolm had very admirably hidden the full malice he surely felt for this wretched man.

Banquo's laugh was strangled. "My son will be earl, she said. Not me." He squeezed his eyes shut.

Malcolm cast a concerned look at the boy and frowned down at Banquo. "Do not tell me ye were chasing after that old witch's tale? Macbeth has discounted it. Why could ye not do so?"

A witch's tale? She tried to catch Malcolm's attention, but he was focused on Banquo, whose eyes burned with an answering hatred toward the younger man. Such a shame for him to die in a state of malevolence. Perhaps she should, after all, escort the boy out.

"Macbeth shall be Earl of Menteith, and my son after him," Banquo said.

"I don't care about the title, father," the boy said. "Don't die. If you die, we will have n-no one."

Marielle hesitated, and then went to stand behind Giles, setting a hand to his shoulder. The boy didn't seem to notice.

"But ye weren't content to wait for the prophecy?" Malcolm said. "Ye say ye killed Macbeth? Why not just attempt to kill me? Why concoct the story of my illegitimacy?"

"Not a story. It's true. Lady Fiona knows it."

The boy's shoulders shook under her touch, and she felt his silent sobbing. Tears formed in her own eyes, and she pressed them back, sighing. The evidence Banquo sought, if there was any, would be the letters she'd handed Malcolm. Thank God she would never have to share them with this villain.

Malcolm glanced at the boy. "Is your mother dead?"

Giles nodded.

"And your kin? Grandparents, uncles, aunts?"

"I have only my brother. If I have my brother."

"What arrangements have ye made for these lads?" he asked Banquo.

Banquo's eyelids fluttered and he mumbled something unintelligible.

"Ye're not alone, lad," Malcolm said gruffly. "Ye have a cousin: me." He pursed his lips. "Two cousins, me and Macbeth's daughter, Lucie. Your father hasn't claimed to have killed her. Providing ye don't try to stab me again ye'll come live with me and learn how to be a gentleman and if need be, an earl. I'll look after ye, your brother and Lucie as well."

"And so will I," Marielle said.

Malcolm blinked and looked up at her, his face softening. "Yes." He nodded. "We none of us will be alone. Banquo, I'm claiming this lad. The older one as well."

Banquo's eyelids fluttered again, and Marielle saw the tiniest of nods.

She let out a long breath. Perhaps Banquo was not irredeemable. And yet the world, and this boy would be better off without him.

"Giles," Marielle whispered. "If you have anything to say to him, do so now." She squeezed the boy's shoulder.

Malcolm beckoned her out of the room, and Wythe stepped in to take over the watch.

She let herself be led into the corridor, fighting the inevitable heaviness that came with a dying.

Perhaps sensing her mood, Malcolm stopped and leaned close, his breath feathering her cheek. "'Tis not the proper time, I suppose, but I must ask: did ye just propose marriage to me, Comtesse?"

Marriage? The impulse to help the boy had been just that—an impulse of the moment.

But marriage? She clapped a hand over her mouth, fighting both a smile and sudden tears. "Is that why you said yes, Malcolm?"

He wrapped her in an embrace. "A woman who wears trousers might be so bold. But ye know, I have little to offer, being a bastard."

She shook her head against his still-damp coat. "You are the Earl of Menteith. It was sheer madness for him to think he could steal the title. I feel pity for the boy, but not for the man. Whoever stabbed him has done the world a favor."

She looked up into troubled eyes. "Do I sound too ruthless?"

"Did I?"

"No. If he were to live, we would have to summon the justice of the peace to bring charges, instead of merely recording his death."

He frowned, and emotion shone in his eyes. He was remembering the murders Banquo had confessed.

"What is Greer to you, truly?"

"A friend. A good friend. I can't think that she's dead, or Macbeth. He was always larger than life."

"You must write a letter to your aunt," she said. "I'll have a man carry it."

"I will do that directly. As soon as..." He tipped her chin up and pressed a gentle kiss to her lips. "We ought to keep watch with the lad."

She nodded. She was in grave danger of losing her heart.

Or perhaps, she already had.

CHAPTER NINE

A Wee Letter

Three days later
5 April, 1815

"What will you do with me now, sir?" Giles asked as he and Malcolm rode back to Bloodmoor Hill Manor after the simple internment in the parish graveyard.

After a long night of suffering, death had finally come for Banquo Monday morning. Marielle had sent Giles home with Wythe and Twyla, and had summoned the local squire who served as both justice of the peace and coroner. The fat lazy fellow had accepted a bottle of brandy and the theory that Banquo, enroute to Yarmouth, had lost his way and, having caught a chill during the terrible storm, sought refuge at her home. 'Twas a blessing the squire liked Marielle's brandy so well. He'd found no need to inspect the body and quickly ruled that death resulted from illness, with no inquest required.

Giles had grieved quietly, likely worrying about his brother and brooding upon everything that had transpired since the older lad left him to travel to London.

"Were ye happy at school?" Malcolm asked, taking a stab at both finding an answer to the lad's question and drawing him out.

He chewed on his lower lip. "When my brother was there it was tolerable."

"I had one or two friends who made school bearable. We shall either find your brother or learn his fate. Our cousin Macbeth's as well." He'd sent an express to his Aunt Fiona, telling her of Banquo's death and asking for news of Macbeth, Greer, and Banquo's older son. "Meanwhile, ye'll travel with us to Yarmouth tomorrow, where we'll await a reply from my aunt. After that, ye may return to school, or travel to France with us." If Macbeth and Greer truly were dead, he might have to summon Lucie as well.

"Are you going to fight Bonaparte?"

Stories were trickling in that Bonaparte had won the allegiance of the French military and was planning to reestablish his empire. In Austria, Prussia, the Low Countries, and England, troops were mobilizing to oppose him.

England had been at war for most of Malcolm's life. As heir to an earldom, he'd not been expected to join up.

But he was a Highlander. He ought to be fighting. He wanted to fight.

"We shall see," he said. "I'm going because the Comtesse says I must look into my mother's family's estates. Apparently, my mother was the granddaughter of a duke."

Unimpressed, the lad pursed his lips and said "I don't want to be earl."

"Perhaps fate won't require that of ye, Giles. Know that, even if we find your brother hale and hearty, I don't plan to surrender Menteith just yet. I must see what's what in France, and meanwhile, I have competent men tending to the business at home."

"You and the Comtesse might have a son."

Giles was still fashing over the earldom. "We're not married, lad."

Nor had he yet bedded her. Not for lack of desire, his or hers. They'd shared no more than a few stolen kisses.

And rightly so. A man had just died, and they couldn't make light of that man's son's grief.

She was a fine woman, the Comtesse. Efficient, self-contained, and not given to dramatic displays, Marielle was nevertheless thoughtful of the lad's pain. She'd seen to the death certificate, promised to arrange the funeral, and then packed Malcolm off to post his letters. He'd arrived in Lowestoft so late that he'd spent the night in the inn there.

The lad's grief made his own sorrows seem pale by comparison. For all of his childhood, he'd had a loving father. And now, mayhap, he'd have a loving woman.

He yearned to know Marielle better. And yes, to marry her, if she would have him.

"'Tis true though," he said. "We might have a son."

"Is she... is she quite respectable?"

"The Comtesse?"

The lad nodded.

"My chosen lady? Ye are a bold one, Giles." He shook his head. "And as to that, I'll only say, she is French."

Giles's frown made him laugh. "She's been through many trials in her life, but I believe she's honorable. Not the same, perhaps as respectable, but far more important."

***

After an early dinner prepared by the neighbor's wife, Marielle produced a map and they went over the plans for the next day's travel. The road to Fenwick on Sea and the Queen's Barque was said to be still flooded, but on his visit to Lowestoft, he'd scouted the local farm tracks. Wythe had offered his cart to freight Marielle's trunk, and at Lowestoft they would change to the post chaise Malcolm had arranged to carry them and their baggage onward to Yarmouth.

With all of Giles' questions answered, Marielle sent the lad off to bed and fetched a bottle of brandy, pouring two glasses and seating herself in the chair next to his.

For dinner that night, she'd donned a second fine dress, this one a deep blue like her eyes.

"And how did ye manage to fasten that dress, my lady?" he asked.

"I enlisted Twyla's help while the chickens were roasting."

"We shall have to arrange a maid for ye."

"Oh? Will we need a valet also?" Her fingers interlaced his. "Or shall we simply help each other to dress?"

"Come here." He tugged her onto his lap and spent the next few minutes at last ardently kissing her until she broke away, stroking his jaw.

"You shaved again."

"Yes. I'm perfectly capable of shaving and dressing myself. But ye're a Comtesse, and we'll hire a maid for ye in Yarmouth. Or perhaps in Calais when we land. That will probably be wiser. A French maid will be less shocked about us sharing a bed." Unless they married first. He would get to that subject.

"I thought, perhaps, you might have changed your mind."

He traced a finger over her bosom. "No."

"Every night, I expected a knock on my door."

They'd spent the first night on Banquo's death watch. The second night he'd been at the inn in Lowestoft. And last night he'd found an empty guest room and collapsed.

"I arrived here in the wee hours of the morning. When I looked in on ye, ye were snoring."

She gave him a playful smack. "This will be my last night at Bloodmoor Hill Manor."

"Ye have memories here. Are ye sad to be leaving?"

"That is not my point. My point is that I told you I have a bed."

"I slept on a bed last night."

"Not my comfortable bed."

He laughed. "Giles asked me today if ye are quite respectable."

"I'm not, of course. I am a widow."

"And French."

"Yes."

"Thank heavens. Will ye marry me, Marielle?"

She cocked her head and eyed him. "Perhaps."

"Perhaps?" He settled a hand just under her breast and pulled her closer.

"I will give you an answer... after."

"After?"

She smiled her siren's smile and wiggled, trying to stand. "Come. I have been a wife already, and there were... aspects lacking. You must convince me that marrying you will offer advantages that will make up for the loss of my freedom."

He scooped her into his arms and got to his feet.

She squeaked. "There is no need to be any more dashing than you already are. And you may injure yourself."

"Ye've thrown down a challenge, my love."

"Your *love*...oh my." She chuckled against his ear. "*Très galant*, my lord. I may faint before—"

He stopped her lips with another kiss, then stomped up the stairs and down the corridor to a door, entering the empty chamber she'd first led him to.

The letters were still in his coat pocket. He'd taken them out a few times and looked at them, and then put them back unread.

Huffing, he carried her through to the sitting room, then into the chamber that Marielle had disappeared into the first night.

Eyes adjusting to the dark, he made out the ghostly shapes of chairs and tables. And a tester bed. Not one worthy of royalty but large enough for two people if they were sufficiently intertwined. That thought and the lush bundle of woman he carted brought his privy counsellor to full alert.

But he wouldn't rush his fences, not if an agreement to marry depended on his skills.

"Ye promised a big bed," he teased.

"I did not. I promised a comfortable bed. Put me down."

He took a few steps more, dropped her onto the bed and landed on his forearms, pinning her under him.

"This?" she hissed. "This is romance?"

He dipped his head and captured her lips, tasting brandy and a hint of expensive perfume. Her arms circled his neck, pulling him closer, cushioning him on her breasts. Freeing a hand, he dipped a finger into the low bodice, exploring.

With a nudge at his chest, she released him and tugged at his neckcloth, untying it, while he slid her bodice down and fondled the tips of her breasts, wondering if her color was rising.

He had to see her.

He stood and tore off the loosened neckcloth. Marielle propped herself on her elbow.

"Candles," he said. "Light." He walked toward the mantel, stumbling against furniture with a crude oath.

"I will help you."

He heard the rustle of skirts as she hurried after him. His hand landed on the tinderbox before hers, and he caught her up to him for a quick kiss before grabbing a branch of candles and carrying them to the bedside table.

The scent of her perfume muddling him, he fumbled the tinder and flint like a schoolboy until she tenderly took everything from his hands.

"There is a lamp on a cabinet over there," she said, pointing.

The breathlessness in her voice stirred him more and he found her lips again, pressing her to him and trailing kisses over the warm pulse at her neck.

"Come to bed," she whispered.

He heard the plop of the flint as she dropped it and remembered the candles, setting her back from him. "Light the candles and I'll fetch the lamp. Ye may be the Comtesse of Midnight but I want to see all of ye."

He walked in the direction she'd pointed, being more careful of obstacles, and returned with the lamp.

The first taper of candlelight made her face glow, and the next turned her hair to spun bronze, and then another highlighted her pale breast tipped by a puckered rosebud.

He twirled her around, unhooking her dress, loosening her stays, and then pausing for another long kiss.

She shoved at him. "Let us be done with this clothing."

In a flurry, they shed clothing, watching each other until she wore only her stockings and garters.

His breath caught. She was beautiful, all womanly curves, as he'd suspected, like one of Botticelli's revelers. He reached for her, but she grasped his hand before he could touch her, and swept him with a gaze from head to foot, back up, and then down to settle on the proof of his desire.

"Are ye finding my aspects lacking?" he asked.

She smiled, and then laughed, walking into his arms. "Let us see what happens next. Perhaps I shall *have* to marry you."

***

As the candles burned lower, Marielle stroked the hair on Malcolm's chest, watching his slumber. He'd proved to be a more generous and far more effective lover than either her lieutenant or Gaspar.

But could she marry him? Would he, after they arrived in Yarmouth, after he heard from his aunt, would *he* want to marry *her*?

Likely not, and the thought saddened her. She felt pity for herself, certainly, because she'd be alone again, but also for Malcolm who would go on alone with so many responsibilities. And he would fulfill them, that she knew, even though, like that poor child down the hall, his world had been pulled out from under him.

The generous impulse to take charge of Giles—that had made her heart fill with love for Malcolm. With certainty that she must be with him.

Which she had quickly tried very hard to dash, of course, because she was, after all, a hardened cynic. Malcolm might feel that after tonight's interlude marriage was required as a matter of honor—and how rare a notion was that for a young man of three and twenty taking an older widow as a lover?

He wasn't a fool, and he wasn't a virgin either. Malcolm was a puzzle, an old soul in a young virile body.

Had he read the letters she'd given him yet? She'd asked him about them on Monday, and he mumbled something about reading them later, just before mounting his horse and riding off to Lowestoft.

A hand came down over hers. “Ye’re awake,” he said.

“I cannot sleep when my vision is filled with so much beauty.”

He opened his eyes and frowned. “I didn’t satisfy ye.”

He had. More than once. “It has been a long time for me. I fear you will find me insatiable.”

His arms snaked around her. “I am ready to rise to the occasion. However, I fear I’ve barely slept in the past five days.”

“Then sleep now.”

“Ye’re fashing about aught.”

“What?”

“Something’s troubling ye.”

She couldn’t tell him her worries. The Comtesse of Midnight, as he had called her, would never fear losing a man’s love, would she? “I am curious about the letters. Have you read them?”

“I’ve been too... too...”

“Afraid?”

He flung an arm over his eyes. “Highlanders are not afraid of wee letters.”

She scuttled over him and jumped off the bed, retrieving his coat and the letters she knew would be tucked inside. He hadn’t broken either seal.

She caught him watching, propped on one arm, his eyes drinking her in, his gaze making her insides melt.

"Careful," she said. "I will start making demands on you if you look at me like that." She placed the letters on his chest, moved the still-unlit lamp closer, and used one of the candles to light it.

"You must read them."

"Ye're a bossy one."

"Perhaps I am older and wiser. I know that a wound not tended will fester and never heal." She grabbed a pillow. "Sit up."

He complied, and she popped the pillow in behind him.

"I've been most curious about these letters since I found them in Gaspar's hiding place. I don't believe he gave Banquo anything more than a story. Now. I shall give you some privacy."

He grabbed her hand and tugged her on top of him. Her breasts brushed the letters while his eyes grew smoky and dark.

She put a finger to his lips and rolled off of him. "Read first. I will lie here and be silent."

He let out a long breath and then cracked the seal of the thicker letter and unfolded it. A smaller, finer piece of paper was enclosed that looked suspiciously like a bank draft. He bit his lip over that, and then turned to the letter, written on a heavy trimmed foolscap. The handwriting was terse and inelegant, surely a man's, and the note brief—one page, with wide margins and spacing. Malcolm skimmed the words, frowning.

He broke the second seal. This was also a brief missive, but in a finer, more elegant hand.

Still frowning, he folded them both and set them aside.

"Well?" she asked, rolling to face him.

"There is a bank draft from twenty years past for five thousand pounds." His gaze went to the canopy. "Untouched."

"What did they say?"

"Everyone is sorry."

"Your mother?"

"And my father. But he told me at the end that he was sorry, along with telling me the prophecy. Though he never said precisely what he was sorry for."

She sat up, remembering the other thing she was curious about. "The witch's tale you mentioned to Banquo?"

"Do ye always remember everything?"

"Yes. Will you share it with me?"

He flung an arm over his eyes again, as if it was all finally too much for him—prophecies, letters, apologies, a madman chasing him across England.

"But only if you wish," she added.

He reached for her then and she clasped his hand.

"When they were boys, my father, Macbeth, and Banquo stumbled across an old woman at a bothy stirring a cauldron."

"A bothy?"

"A... a hut. A small cottage. Father was young, yet already he was Earl of Menteith.

She told him Macbeth would be earl after him, and that Banquo's son would be earl after Macbeth."

"You weren't yet born."

"No. And my mother—his wife, I suppose she was, not my mother—couldn't give him an heir. I suppose the marriage soured, and he began an affair with my mother. When I was born, they passed me off as his son by his wife. She died when I was very young, like the last Comtesse. I didn't know her. After that, it was always only me and my father."

It was astonishing. "Scotland has divorce, does it not? Why not just divorce his wife and marry... Oh."

"Yes. There was no easy way for her to be rid of the Comte."

"Your father had more scruples than Banquo. Had he not, my fate may have changed and I would never have married the Comte, and we might never have met." She snuggled closer. "But the prophecy... We do not have to marry, my love" she said. "It will only complicate things if we have a son..."

She caught her breath. She was jumping ahead to children. Well and why not since she knew the consequences of the love-making they'd just engaged in. But, children with Malcolm... The thought filled her heart so much that she wanted to weep.

She found herself in fact weeping, and in his arms, where he held her, shushing her. "If we have a son, we'll raise him together."

"Or a daughter."

"Or both." His hand moved over her back slowing and finally stopping, and his breathing became regular. The letters beckoned for her to read them, but there would be time for them. There would be time for many things, if they were lucky.

She reached over him and blew out the candles, and then nestled into his arms and slept.

EPILOGUE

At the Blue Boar

"Well?" Marielle asked, peering over Malcolm's shoulder.

"They are all alive." He whooped with uncharacteristic enthusiasm.

She was learning that her lover was a serious man, though not without kindness, and not without humor.

"Giles, ye don't have to be earl," he said. "Your brother lives, as well as Macbeth and Greer."

Giles grinned from his place at the table, where he was having his second helping of the inn's good breakfast.

They'd arrived at the Blue Boar in Yarmouth the day before, Malcolm having left instructions at the inn in Lowestoft to forward all mail with urgency. They'd been fortunate to find a suite of three rooms available and had been preparing to go out to shop for their journey when the letter arrived.

"Does it say where Fleance is?" Giles asked.

Fleance was the improbable Scottish name borne by Giles's brother, poor lad.

"He's with Macbeth and Greer, all of them still very much alive."

He and Giles shared happy smiles. Malcolm's glance her way showed his relief. Banquo's lie had caused him a good deal of needless concern.

"They are all still in Chelsea, but will leave soon for Deal. Macbeth is to meet there and join the Highland regiment being brought over from Cork."

"Can we go there, sir?"

"Let me see." Malcolm scanned more of the letter. "He and the regiment are traveling from Deal to Ostend in a week or two." He smiled again at the boy. "He's bringing Greer, Lucie, and your brother."

Marielle saw the excitement in his eyes. She knew that Greer and Lucie had been his only family these last few years, and they would be reunited. He was also glad to have Banquo's boys reunited, and to learn that his cousin still lived. They were all his newly acquired family.

And where did that leave her? Except for her elderly husband, she'd been alone for so very long.

His arm came around her, his face suddenly serious. "The Highlanders will fight under Wellington," he said. "Greer and Lucie plan to follow the drum."

Malcolm had admitted he wished to offer his services. For all her talk about fighting Napoleon, she prayed that the army wouldn't take him.

But he was a man truly grown, and must be free to choose, and for her part, she must swallow her worries and hope that his newly acquired family might also be hers. Life might be short, and she must take whatever blessings she found. And if Malcolm was to fight, she would most certainly follow the drum as well.

"We must make sail for Ostend," she said, "and not Calais. Giles, you must have new shirts and neck cloths and I daresay smalls before we travel. Go scratch out a note to your brother, and then fetch your coat and hat, and you and I will visit the shops while Malcolm writes a longer letter and arranges our transport."

The boy loped off into his adjoining bedchamber.

"Is there any bad news?" she asked, sensing his mood.

"Only the tale of how Banquo got his wound. He tossed Greer into the Thames. She managed to stab him and pull him in with her. They thought he'd drowned."

"Oh," she said, hope rising in her. Besides being, like herself, not quite respectable, Greer was a woman of substance. "I look forward to meeting the rest of your family."

"They will be your family as well, Marielle."

He smiled and opened his arms, and she went to him.

The End

A Note from the Author

I hope you've enjoyed Malcolm and Marielle's story.

Malcolm first appeared in *Fated Hearts*, my retelling of the Macbeth story for the Tragic Characters in Classic Lit Project. When the Bluestocking Belles offered me the opportunity to join them in the Storm & Shelter Collection, I knew it was a perfect opportunity to have Malcolm find his own happily-ever-after.

Researching the story introduced me to Suffolk and more importantly Norfolk, a county which makes an appearance in the third story in this Macbeth series, *Claims of the Heart*, the story of Macbeth's daughter Lucie, available in spring 2022.

Many thanks go to the Bluestocking Belles. Working with them has been a privilege and a joy.

At this point in my note to readers, I always express my gratitude to my husband for his unfailing support of my writing, which takes me away from family life for hours at a time. Sadly, he passed away in October 2021. He wanted me to keep writing; I hope that I can, and I hope that his selfless love, generosity, and strength will find their way into every one of my heroes.

I love hearing from readers! Please follow me on Facebook, Bookbub, Pinterest, and at my website, AlinaKField.com. And for monthly news about releases and sales, sign up for my newsletter at my website. I promise I won't spam you or sell your email address!

Best regards and happy reading!

Alina K. Field

p.s.: Read on for excerpt from *Fated Hearts* and *Claims of the Heart*.

Fated Hearts

London
Friday, 3 March, 1815

A crush was what they called these suffocating occasions, and the term was apt.

Major Finnley Macbeth, Scottish baron and late of his majesty's Highland Brigade, shifted his weight from the leg that still ached like the devil, and scanned the room for his quarry, an undersecretary in the Home Office who he'd met at the army's winter quarters in Frenada.

From his spot near a damask covered wall, he measured each breath, trying to calm his rising unease. The heavy scent of perfume mixed with fine beeswax and hothouse florals unsettled more than his stomach. The shimmering silks and waving plumes threatened to stir the disquieting visions plaguing him lately.

Fire, explosions, rain, the screams of men and horse.

He squeezed his hands into fists. These were not the hellish memories of the recent past, dammit, but rattling visions of some battle yet to come.

Or not. Foretelling the future was for Travellers and crones, wasn't it? Not battle-hardened men like himself.

He inhaled slowly, holding the breath for a count, and then eased the air out. Best keep his purpose in mind—he was here to track down Sir Thomas Abernathy, lately arrived in London, and rumored to be attending this rout.

His gaze swept the room, seeking the distinctive bald pate. In spite of his own forty-three years, his eyesight was still keen enough to make out a sniper or spot the dust of a fleeing stag. Keen enough as well to relish the deep décolletages and clinging, delicate, almost transparent skirts on display this night, a vision far more cheering than the one the Sight was showing him.

A more modestly clad woman stood alone halfway across the ballroom, her back turned to him, surveying the room as he was doing.

A memory stabbed him, laced with an old shame. He'd once known a lass with hair like this, so abundant, so near to black. The lady tonight had crowned all the loveliness with dark feathers, like a glorious cormorant. His hand itched to pull out those feathers and rake his hands through the tumble of hair, as he'd once done...

He caught a steadying breath. It couldn't be her. He'd simply been without a woman too long.

And these visions plaguing him of he knew not what? That foolishness grew from naught but fatigue, the wages of war, and the steady company of too much death. Napoleon had been defeated. He must put the memories of battle and that more distant passion aside. The lovely lady with feathers atop her head was only a stranger wondering where her man had got to.

Yet he couldn't turn away. As he watched, she pivoted one way, and then the other, allowing a glimpse of dangling earbobs and a firm chin.

Drawn to her, he stepped out on his bad leg just as she turned.

Pain shot through his hip. The room threatened to fall away but he held onto the pain, let it shore him up whilst he swore a silent curse.

It *was* her.

Earlier that evening

As the lights of London came into view, Greer Douglas smoothed the silk skirt of her evening gown and glanced out the coach window again. "I wondered if we should be quite safe traveling so late at night." Chelsea seemed such a great distance from Mayfair, though at home in Scotland, she'd often journeyed farther back and forth on market day.

Her companion grunted. "I'd rather have stayed home and read the proposed Corn Law. Not to mention that it is Lent."

Greer would have chuckled, had she not been so nervous. Malcolm Comyn, Earl of Menteith, was a sober young man, but not a pious one. "We are in England now, Malcolm, two fish out of water and we must learn to swim. As long as we don't have to surrender my new earbobs to a highwayman."

"Aunt Fiona read the tea leaves and felt the coachman and groom shall be adequate protection." He patted her hand. "Do not ye worry, Cousin. I'm not wholly incapable of handling a dirk and a pistol. Though I had rather not."

"Ye had rather not mingle, either."

"So true. But Aunt Fiona insisted we must honor her friend by attending this affair, and so we are here."

Lady Fiona Carlin, who'd been widowed longer than Greer's thirty-eight years, had surprised them both at breakfast with this invitation to her friend's small gathering. The elderly lady did not herself feel up to attending. Nor would Lady Fiona allow Greer's daughter, Lucie, to attend until she had made her come-out.

When that would be, was anyone's guess. Poor Lucie. At the age of almost twenty, she was anxious to experience more of London, especially the social events of the *ton*.

Greer feared that her daughter's manners needed further refinement. Like her mother, Lucie was a country girl, unused to higher society. Life had smoothed out most of her own rough edges, but Lucie was often too direct, too outspoken. And her temper...

Greer pressed a hand to her chest and tried to breathe through the bad memories. Lucie's temper was an inherited gift from the father who had never met her.

"I suppose that honoring her friend is the least we can do to repay your aunt's hospitality," she said.

Two weeks after Malcolm's departure from Scotland, a letter had arrived for Greer from Lady Fiona inviting her and Lucie to join Malcolm as her guests for the London season. She'd even sent the means for hiring a chaise and post riders.

Greer had made up her mind to write back declining—Malcolm would not want his irksome relations crowding him in London. But as she read on, Lady Fiona mentioned the upcoming celebrations of the end of two decades of war, and the latest gossip.

And among the items of gossip she'd included the tidbit that Major Finnley Macbeth had arrived in London.

The time would come when they would speak—and just let her have a piece of him. But not tonight. Tonight, she wanted to see how the great world of London would welcome a woman like herself.

When their carriage jerked to its final stop in front of the brightly lit townhouse, Malcolm handed her out, and escorted her through the receiving line where their elderly hostess, Lady Estelle Walby, looked her over with a gleam in her eye that matched Lady Fiona's.

And then Malcolm abandoned her.

"I must step away to the gentleman's," he said, with his usual bluntness. "Where will I find ye?"

"Since I don't know a soul, I'll seek out Lady Estelle when she's free."

He shook his head. "Proceed to the middle of the room, and I'll find ye there shortly."

"Yes, my lord," she teased.

Wandering deeper into the room, she scanned the groupings of people. Not one familiar face. Not one. At home, in the Highlands, she'd know every soul at a local assembly.

Oh, but the gowns were far more magnificent here. The glow from the candelabra gleamed off exquisite jewels and sparkled in mirrors arranged to brighten the room. Large urns filled with roses and gladioli stood on pillars, and along one wall, chaperones kept eagle eyes on girls Lucie's age. Some of the young ladies looked as nervous as herself.

Across the room, she caught the curious gaze of three young bucks. One whispered to the other. She lifted her chin and turned fully around.

And for one desperate moment her heart stopped, and then started up again in a wild gallop.

A man stood watching her, a tall, broad chested man in a gold waistcoat and a fine dark coat, golden-eyed and handsome, with hair flaming in bright tones of red, hair pulled back into an old-fashioned queue, hair that used to fall to strong shoulders in wild tangled waves.

Finnley was here.

***

How had she not aged? was his first thought. Twenty years had slipped away, but her beauty hadn't. The most beautiful girl he'd ever seen. She was the same: her raven hair, her glorious bosom, her stubborn chin and the deep blue of her eyes.

Eyes that used to look at him as if he was one of the old gods. Before. Before she...

He caught his breath battling a surge of stinging emotion. What was the truth?

Desire for her flooded him. If he could but hold her again. If he could restore them to what they'd once—

A gentleman pushed through the crowd and joined her. Dark-haired and manly, 'twas Duncan.

Numbness settled over him. He ought to turn around and depart. By all that was holy, Duncan should have died of his wounds after their long-ago duel, but here he was, looking hale, with a braw strength that...

The man followed the line of Greer's sight, and his eyes met Finnley's.

This wasn't Duncan, but he was very much like him. Greer had found another.

Or had she? He was much younger, this buck, pushing himself up next to the lady. A couple passed into Finnley's line of vision.

He slid sideways, too quickly; his wounded leg seized, and he stumbled, catching himself on a footman who managed to juggle his tray of drinks and Finnley's weight.

"Damnation," he said, apologizing and thanking the servant. "Game leg," he muttered.

Face heating, he glanced back. It was too late for an orderly retreat. His ex-wife was advancing upon him, her young pup in tow.

At Finnley's stumble, Greer gave into instinct, and a mite of courage, and walked straight toward him, trusting that Malcolm would follow. Malcolm had been a mere bairn in those early days so long ago. He'd never met Finnley Macbeth, the man who'd almost made him lord of Menteith before his voice had changed.

Was Finnley already in his cups tonight? He'd been a young man much given to the whisky. And his face was aflame. Probably with anger.

No matter. As she drew closer, her resolve hardened. Now that she was in London, now that she'd found him, now that her feet were moving, she would ensure that Finnley Macbeth would meet and acknowledge his child. Not tonight, certainly, but soon. It would be done, at the point of a blade if need be. He would see that he'd never been cuckolded, that she'd never betrayed him, that Lucie was his. Not for her own sake, but for Lucie's.

As she neared him, he pulled himself up in his proud manner and dipped his head in a poor semblance of a bow, raising her ire. Pausing before him, she lifted her chin and gathered what dignity she could muster, hoping to belie the heat rising into her cheeks. In the past twenty years he'd grown into braw, mature manhood, and he still had the ability to stir her.

This close, she could see a scar tracing the side of his face, not fresh, but not terribly old either. Finnley with his hot temper and sense of his own power would be riddled with scars, wouldn't he?

She dipped in the slightest of curtsies and said "Sir."

"Madam."

The gruff voice was thick with emotion, triggering her own answering flood of moisture.

She swallowed it down. There'd be no weeping, at least not on her part.

"Greer." That was Malcolm, at her elbow, chiding her.

Finnley's hot gaze shifted, and his mouth firmed. He gave another head bob. "I am—"

"Macbeth," she said. "Finnley Macbeth, Baron of Calder."

Tension rippled from him. "Major Macbeth," he said, in the sort of tight voice he might have used before a fight.

She gritted her teeth. "And this gentleman is Malcolm Comyn, since last year, Earl of Menteith. Duncan's boy, all grown up."

Not a man to hide his emotions, was Finnley. Surprise chased the anger from his face only to be followed by something that looked like...shame? Could it be?

His shoulders dropped and he dipped his head again. "You'll know who I am then, Lord Menteith."

The two men exchanged a long look.

"'Tis perhaps not exactly a pleasure to make your acquaintance, sir," Finnley said, "Yet I'm glad of it anyway." He turned his golden eyes on her. "And glad to see ye looking so well Lady Menteith."

She gasped. "I am not—"

"Greer is not and has never been Lady Menteith," Malcolm said. "She's neither my wife, my stepmother, nor, may I add, in case ye're wondering, my mistress."

His forthright speech made her cheeks flame. Other eyes were turning their way.

"Put any such notion aside." Malcolm went on with his usual thoroughness. "We are kin, distant cousins. And she goes by the name Greer Douglas, Mrs. Greer Douglas, for to be called a Miss seems an injustice, Major Macbeth."

All the old hurts washed over her, the old shame rising. Spurning Macbeth's surname, she'd returned to her own name, but had adopted the missus, for the sake of her daughter.

Finnley's face drained of color, becoming as white as parchment, his abundant freckles in stark relief, only his scar blazing. For once, she wished Malcolm were not so direct. He'd left them both speechless and tongue-tied.

Before either of them could muster words, a man wedged his way through the crowd and stood beside Finnley. A hale and handsome enough man, he was, thickly dark-haired with a splash of distinctive white that streaked back from a peak at the top of his forehead.

She knew this man, another apparition from far in the past, one she'd rather not see. Giles Banquo, was another distant cousin to Malcolm and Finnley.

"Who have we here?" Banquo exclaimed. "Why, it's Gr—that is...I'm unsure what to call you. And is that Menteith, all grown up?

And...Macbeth, is that you? I heard you were gravely wounded at Toulouse."

A flicker of emotion passed through Finnley, quickly shuttered. He greeted Banquo coldly, as did Malcolm. She dipped her head, unable to speak. Finnley had been gravely wounded? Lucie might not have had a chance to meet him.

In spite of the cold reception Banquo chattered on. He was said to have once been a good friend to Duncan. And yet he'd once been a good friend to Duncan's enemy, Finnley, too. In those days, he'd been another minor Scottish baron like Finnley, but he'd left Scotland not long after Finnley's departure. Any other news she'd received about him had been filtered and screened by her villainous aunt and cousins.

Her hands fisted in her new silk gloves. 'Twas another bad memory, one that she must not ever forget. She would never be that young, trusting, girl again.

She wouldn't trust others, nor could she entirely trust herself or her own instincts. Silky manners, sureness of belief, none of those could be relied on. In her youth, she'd not been able to see that. Nor had Macbeth.

They'd both been too young, too proud, too much in love. Until he'd stopped loving her and cast her away.

"I should be pleased to join you," Finnley said.

Join who? Drat, but while she was woolgathering in the last century, they'd made some arrangement or other.

"Why don't I come along, as well," Banquo said. "I've a new mount. Anxious to put him through his paces. I say, Macbeth, do you still have the gray you were riding at Madrid?"

While Finnley uttered a terse "no," Malcolm cast Banquo a stony gaze, then offered Greer his arm. "Come along, Cousin, our hostess is now free."

Finnley's eyes flashed with something that looked very much like longing.

Was that wishful thinking on her part? Foolish woman that she was. She swallowed her own answering surge of emotion and dipped her head, tongue-tied again.

Somehow, someday, somewhere—not tonight, and not here of course—she must dredge up her courage and confront the man.

Malcolm led her off, and as it turned out, he was not entirely unknown in this crowd. He'd secured a membership at White's, and several men greeted him. He introduced Greer to them and, in some cases, the wives who'd accompanied them.

'Twas curiosity that made her an object of interest and had them queueing up. The *ton* would be speculating whether she was more than a cousin to Malcolm. True it was as well, that though her personal scandal was twenty years in the past, divorce was uncommon enough for old muck to be dug up for a fresh flow of gossip. Finnley's presence here would ensure that it would be.

Was that why Lady Fiona had insisted they come? If so, she was in truth glad for it. She was ready to face the *ton*'s worst.

Malcolm's aunt had been surprisingly kind, welcoming Greer and Lucie, two strangers, and yet, as it turned out, distantly related to her by marriage. The lady's late husband had been kin to the Naughtons, the aunt and cousins who'd taken Greer in when her parents died. They'd never ever so much as mentioned Lady Fiona or her husband, unusual for her cousin, who'd been the sort to pursue any advantageous connection. The only reason the Naughtons had taken in a shameful divorcee had been the chance to dip into her dowry.

A man spoke, pulling her out of more woolgathering. She had better attend to the conversation, lest they think she was daft.

One of Malcolm's bachelor friends repeated an invitation for her to ride in the park in his phaeton.

Faith, and the man couldn't be much older than Malcolm's three-and twenty years, certainly no older than thirty. Far more appropriate for Lucie than for herself, not to mention that her life was so jumbled and uncertain now, she had no interest in being courted. Or was an invitation to ride not considered courting?

Goodness. She was as much a goose as any green girl.

She declined the invitation, pleading their residence so far out of town, and made a point of keeping her wits about her for the rest of the evening.

Finnley watched as Greer walked away on young Menteith's arm, his gaze moving to the gentle sway of her hips. Others noticed as well, and Menteith was stopped on the way by male acquaintances seeking to be introduced.

She was no longer his. She wasn't Menteith's either; the lad had made that clear. But she would soon be someone's.

Jealousy nagged at him again. It had been twenty years. Highlanders were not blind to a woman with such beauty and a home of her own. Had she had a man in that time?

Could he make her his again before someone else got to her? She was too fine-looking a woman to be cast to the side for long.

"Well, well," Banquo said quietly. "She's a fine piece. Quite a surprise, isn't it?"

"A fine piece?" he hissed. He tamped down a flare of anger and headed for the door.

"Menteith appearing here with Greer on his arm," Banquo said, dogging him. "A chip off the old block, isn't he?"

Banquo was baiting him. He longed to oblige with his fist, but instead he kept walking, setting his mind to the pain in his limb.

"You're leaving then?" Banquo asked. "Well I may as well leave with you. Safety in numbers, eh? There's whispers the folk will be rioting over these new laws coming."

He'd heard those rumors as well, but at present, his mind was elsewhere.

Find your copy of *Fated Hearts* at all major booksellers.

Claims of the Heart

April 1816
Near Hunstanton, Norfolk

"Two letters arrived for you, my lord."

Tristan Hamilton Howton, Earl of Rudgwick, Major in His Majesty's Horse Guards and a decorated veteran of the Peninsular campaign and Waterloo, extended his arms for Darby to pry the wet coat from his shoulders and ease it over the lump of wood at the end of his right arm.

The valet's disapproving clucks both amused and annoyed him. Mother had tracked down his late father's valet and hired him away from the rich cit he'd been serving. Upon Rudgwick's return from Flanders, Darby had been waiting at Rudgwick Abbey, the ancestral pile in Cambridgeshire, happy to be back serving nobility, yet missing his favored Savile Row haunts.

In Darby's view, Rudgwick Abbey was paradise compared to their present abode, Thornview Farm. With four rooms below, four bedchambers above, and a few small attic rooms for the housekeeper, cook, and two maids, Darby had been sleeping on a cot in the dressing room. Rudgwick's friend, Lord Jeremy Bolton, who had inherited the estate late the previous year from an aunt, was in alt, declaring himself perfectly happy with the cozy cottage and the small income that came with it. And it wasn't entirely a bachelor establishment; Jeremy, too kind and dutiful to ever be a true rake, had offered shelter to another female relative, an elderly cousin and her even older companion.

Rudgwick stepped into clean trousers and held up his arms for Darby's assistance, annoyance niggling at him. He needed a man to tend to his boots, keep his clothing in order, and button his left cuff. Otherwise, he preferred dressing himself, even, or especially, during his time in the army.

"I fear I won't get the salt stains out of those—"

"Yes, yes," Rudgwick said. "A fair day for sailing it was, though, Darby. Are you not glad we're back from touring all the byways of Norfolk?" He'd left Darby behind while he and Jeremy rode hither and yon for the last few weeks, making do with help from inn servants. "Had we supplies on board today we would have made for Inverness."

Jeremy's new home had come with a yacht, a smallish one, in truth, too small for a comfortable journey to Scotland. An old school friend and former naval man, Jeffrey Musbury, had traveled up from his cottage on the River Ware to assess the craft, pronouncing it sound for short days of sailing, and inviting them to join him in summer on the two-master he'd been refurbishing.

Darby made a grumbling noise in his throat and fetched the letters. "A brandy, my lord?"

"Yes." He sighed. There'd be another nagging missive from his fiancée's grandfather, and a lamenting one from his steward.

Darby set a full glass before him. "Shall I break the seals for you, my lord?"

"Why not read them as well," he snapped.

Darby blinked in the way that Mother did before she straightened her shoulders and walked away from his churlishness. The valet was of an age with her, and, like high-born ladies, he'd learned patience and forbearance in the face of surly noblemen.

"Apologies, Darby." It wasn't Darby's or Mother's fault that a French mortar had blown off his hand at Waterloo. "That was uncalled for. Thank you. I shall manage."

Darby dipped his head and left, carrying off the wet and soiled garments.

Rudgwick took a healthy swig of the drink. They'd found cases of spirits in the manor's storeroom, good French brandy, and gin from the Lowlands. It seemed that the free trade reached even the west coast of Norfolk. As pillars of society, he and Jeremy would be expected to support the increased efforts against smuggling, but they had no qualms about availing themselves of Jeremy's late aunt's stores.

He closed his eyes and let the brandy ease the phantom throb in the hand that was no longer there. Then he shuffled the letters one-handed.

One fat missive and one thin. Both had been sent to London, where he was supposed to be in residence, and forwarded on. He broke the seal on the thin one and read.

Sir Thomas Abernathy, a baronet attached to the Home Office, inquired about his health, and asked about his availability to assist with a matter of interest to the Crown. A reply at his earliest convenience would be appreciated.

His curiosity was piqued, but he couldn't help wondering if Mother knew Sir Thomas and if she had put him up to it to orchestrate his return to town.

The second, heftier letter was addressed in a man's scrawl and sent post-paid from Edinburgh.

He hastened to break the seal and flipped to the signature, laughing out loud when he saw who had signed it.

Colonel Finnley Macbeth, Baron of Calder, had written to him. His wife, Greer Macbeth, corresponded with Mother, but the Colonel had never done more than send greetings via those letters.

That called for another dram of brandy.

And then he began to read. A lengthy passage reviewed the Colonel's recovery (he was mending apace), reported on his cousin, Lord Menteith (still in France), and discussed the plans for the two boys Macbeth had taken charge of, his late cousin Banquo's sons. But that was all a prelude for an important request.

> *Your lady mother informs me that you should be in London by now, and so if it would not be an inconvenience to you, I would be much obliged to ask a boon from you. There's a solicitor by the name of Stephenson in the City, who has knowledge of Banquo's business matters. He's failed to reply to several letters, and I can only assume he's ignoring them. I've asked Lucie to pay a call on the man. Lady Fiona has offered help from her man of business, and I've sent Hyde along to London with Lucie.*

Lucie. The name all but leapt from the page. Lucie was in London!

> *However, of late I've had misgivings and worries that, given Banquo's criminal nature, this Stephenson may be a shifty character. Lucie being Lucie, she's likely to find the danger an enticement and plunge ahead. Moreover, I know that a title can often open*

doors that would otherwise remain closed. If you could see your way to offer Lucie assistance, if your new bride has no objections, I would be most grateful.

He read through the letter again and then pulled the bell. As he returned to his seat the door opened.

"That was quick." He turned and saw that it was not a servant, but his host.

Jeremy was a younger and handsomer version of his brother, the Duke of Northam. A handsomer version of Rudgwick as well, with the same height, dark hair, and gray eyes, though they were completely unrelated.

"At your service, my lord," he joked. "The servants are busily preparing for dinner."

"Will you pack my trunk, then?" Rudgwick teased. "Ah, there is Darby, poking his head in behind you. Darby, we are leaving for London in the morning."

"We are?" Jeremy said.

"You may come as well if you wish. I've been summoned to go to the aid of the Crown." *And Lucie Macbeth.*

***

She opened her eyes and came out of the darkness into the red glow of the sun on the horizon and the sound of muffled voices and the chuffing breaths of a struggling horse.

Pegasus had fallen.

Oh, Hades. She must see to him.

Before she could stir, someone loomed over her, her vision too fuzzy to make out who it was. Fear rose in her, and then settled. 'Twas not Jamey Paisley, praise heaven. If he thought to touch her again, she'd... why she'd have a piece of—

"Shhh. Lie still, lass." The voice was one of Menteith Castle's grooms.

Pegasus. How badly was he injured? She pushed at the soft turf, the damp soaking her gloves. The rain had stopped before her ride, but days of downpours had left the soft places soggy and slick, and...

It had been her fault. Jamey's kiss had paled next to that of another man, and then he started to paw, and push, and demand a decision...

She had run and bade him not to follow. Only, she had looked back and seen him mounting.

She'd galloped hard, getting away, running, and running, and running, and then the ground had given way, sliding straight out from under them, and... She lifted her head and pain exploded in it.

"Lie still." A hand touched her shoulder, and she sank back into a dull throbbing.

Velvety grass cushioned her and gave off a sweet odor whilst a breeze tickled her brow, eased the shattering pain and shards of glittering light, and chilled her moist cheeks. She'd been crying and hadn't known it or—she levered a heavy hand and swiped at her face. Her kid glove came back red.

And then... a cloud moved over her. A gloved hand reached for her.

"Oh, my love." Grim lips, shaded by dark scruff formed the words, soundlessly. She heard them in her heart. She knew him there also.

Her hand touched his and she floated up, up, up, into strong arms that settled her onto a soft bed.

"Oh, my love." His lips formed the words again. She couldn't hear the words, but she knew them. She knew.

Stuff and nonsense. Lucie Macbeth, Maid of Calder, blinked the obsessive thoughts away and took in the dizzying view from Lady Estelle Walby's box at Covent Garden. The previous year, she'd attended a play at Drury Lane with her parents, Colonel and Mrs. Finnley Macbeth, Baron and Baroness of Calder. Grand it had been, but not so grand as this, nor so high up.

Truth to tell, she wasn't fond of such heights, which was probably why the vivid memories mixed with imagination were clattering about in her battered head.

This sight, Covent Garden theater, this was a real vision to store away for the long winter nights at home in Calder. All around her the boxes glittered with rich silks, sparkling jewels, and the glint of the glasses of the *ton's* well-to-do spying on other attendees. She must stay right here for the evening instead of wandering about in the past or some unbidden daydream.

"Come along then, ladies." Lady Walby's relation, Lord Grallon, pointed out their plushly appointed seats.

"I haven't attended a performance here since the fire." Lucie's elderly distant cousin, Lady Fiona Carlin, took Lord Grallon's arm and Lucie followed behind them, seating herself at the end of the row next to Lady Fiona. "It's breathtaking. Shall we switch, Lucie, my dear, so you may see the stage better?"

"All the world's the stage here, isn't it, madam?" She'd attended a few glittering balls in Brussels the year before, but nowhere had she seen so many gaily attired ladies. Perhaps it was the matter of the war ending that made the *ton* more festive, as well as the fact that the theater, unlike society balls, was open to people of all ranks. Some of the most beautiful ladies peering out from private boxes would be members of the demimonde.

Lady Walby leaned across Lady Fiona. "You look very well tonight, my dear Lucie. You're sure to catch the eye of the gentlemen. That gown is brilliant."

Lucie murmured a thank you. The gown was, in truth, magnificent. Mother might never have allowed her to wear it. Father would have insisted on a more intrepid escort than the elderly baron, or a large fichu.

Given the bright red of her hair, she herself had been doubtful about this shade of vermilion. When she'd requested a red gown, Lady Fiona and the modiste hadn't dismissed the notion. They'd insisted upon this hue with its rich, almost golden shimmer, and at the first fitting, she'd seen the magic. The richly colored *peau de soia* fabric floated over an underdress of white silk, embroidered, and trimmed in gold, dipping low at the bodice. More gold trimmed the overdress and floated along the tasseled waist and hemline.

She wasn't given to vanity, not much anyway, but tonight she'd found a comely stranger staring back at her from her dressing table mirror. Lady Fiona's maid had twisted her hair up Grecian style, twining faux pearls through the creation that matched the ones at her neck, and teasing out face-framing curls. A light touch of powder had even hidden most of the freckles that were the curse of the ginger-haired.

Catching the eye of the gentlemen wasn't her goal tonight, though it might be a welcome diversion. 'Struth there *was* one gentleman plaguing her thoughts, and he wasn't free. Though she supposed if she encountered him during her sojourn in London, he'd be unable to annoy her as he'd done in Brussels. After all, their only connection was His Majesty's army, and here, they were moving about in different worlds.

In any case, to her knowledge, he wasn't in London. If he appeared tonight at Covent Garden, well, her heart was safely hidden within her vermilion gown, her future was secure in the Calder barony, and she had no need to be wooed. Tomorrow or the next day she would make another attempt to see to her father's business in London. Tonight, she merely wished for the entertaining spectacle of the actors, both on and off the stage.

"And how are the preparations for the grand birthday ball proceeding?" Lady Walby asked.

"Famously." Lady Fiona winked at her. "Isn't that so, Lucie?"

She laughed. "Very true, my lady." She'd turned one and twenty a fortnight before, and Lady Fiona had surprised her by announcing that she was hosting a ball in her honor. "Or so I assume. I can't claim any credit though since Lady Fiona has kept me in the dark about the preparations."

"Tell her, Estelle, that she must have a gown specially made for the occasion. She wants to wear this one again."

"Never turn down an offer of a new gown, my dear." Lady Walby raised her opera glasses. "Oh, do look. Is that not Bridgehampton across from us? And my godson, Lord Jeremy Bolton, with him."

The hair on the back of Lucie's neck quivered and, in no need of an opera glass, she followed the line of vision to the box directly opposite theirs. The Duke of Bridgehampton was a powerful peer, and quite a controlling man as well, if the stories could be believed.

"He's come out of mourning then," Lady Fiona said.

Bridgehampton's son and heir, Marquess Grey, had died several weeks earlier of an unsavory wasting disease brought on by his dissipated life, or so Lucy had surmised from the few details she'd gleaned from her father's servant, Hyde, who was well informed on that sort of gossip.

She'd never seen either man, the duke or his son the marquess, in the flesh, but surely the tall white-haired gentleman was Bridgehampton. The dark-haired young man standing next to him must be Lady Walby's godson.

Unable to turn away, Lucie watched as Bridgehampton remained alert and erect, surveying the vast array of boxes, one by one, until he came to theirs and his eyes landed on her. A jolt went through her. Surely the blasted man didn't know of her, didn't recognize her. Yet if looks might pierce a tender girl's heart, well...

She was no tender girl, though, not after the frights she'd experienced and the horrors she'd seen, and so she sharpened her gaze and thrust back at him, while all else melted away, the only sound being the slow *drub-drub-drub* of her heart beating.

A sharp squeeze of her hand stirred her.

"You are well." Lady Fiona's words were a quiet command, not a question.

Lucie turned and met sparkling topaz eyes so like her own. She often imagined her paternal grandmother might have looked like Lady Fiona. She often wondered if her late grandmother had been plagued with the Sight as well. Not that what she was experiencing, small lapses in time with intense *experiences* and *feelings*, could be called the Sight. After all, she'd suffered a terrible bashing. Her head had been badly concussed... and she'd lost Pegasus.

She hauled herself out of the threatening pit and fixed her attention on the dear lady next to her, forcing a smile. Whatever it was, this so-called gift—curse more like—was so new to her, she craved the guidance of those who had borne the burden longer.

Father might be able to help, but he was in Scotland. She hadn't seen him since this awakening, which started after she left Edinburgh with Lady Fiona.

Besides, she would hate to trouble him by calling to mind his past painful memories, not now that he'd survived the war and reunited with Mother. If Lady Fiona was gifted, as Mother suspected, she might help. It was a mere matter of screwing up the courage to ask. But she wouldn't tell what she was seeing. There was little to tell, memories of the frightful accident being mixed up with glimpses of a man she must never know *that* way, glimpses that were stirring and intimate and absolutely impossible to relate.

The older lady squeezed again and tipped her head toward the opposite box. Lucie glanced over and her heart skipped a beat, and then started racing.

Available in Spring 2022

Books by Alina K. Field

Sons of the Spy Lord Series

Marrying Mr. Gibson

Previously titled *The Bastard's Iberian Bride*

Paulette Heardwyn rushes to visit her dying guardian, set on learning the truth about her father. But the only man with answers takes his secrets to the grave, leaving her penniless—unless she marries his illegitimate son

The Viscount's Seduction

Lady Sirena Hollister has lost everything, even her fey abilities. But when the fairies hand her a chance at a London Season, her schemes for revenge stir up an unknown enemy, and spark danger of a different sort, in the person of a handsome Viscount.

The Rogue's Last Scandal

Falling—literally—into the arms of the *ton*'s most outrageous rogue seems a risky path of escape, but Maria Graciela Kingsley y Romero has no other choice. Only England's greatest spy lord can help her, and he is not to be found—so his son will have to do!

The Counterfeit Lady

Vowing she'll never submit to an arranged marriage, an earl's daughter bolts for the seaside cottage that will someday be hers. But she finds her quiet refuge occupied by the last man she ever wants to see—an American artist, who's also a thief. And, quite possibly one of her father's spies.

Avenging the Earl's Lady

The long war is over, but honor requires vanquishing one last enemy, and the Earl of Shaldon has no time for romance. But when the lady he longs for interferes in his plot, and his enemy strikes at her, nothing else matters but avenging his lady.

Novellas and Holiday Stories

The Marquess and the Midwife

A Christmas Novella
Finalist, 2016 National Reader's Choice Award

Uncovering a lie drives a new marquess back from a self-imposed exile at Christmas to find the only woman he's ever loved. Finding her turns out to be easy, uncovering her stunning secrets, a bit harder. But winning her back will be the greatest challenge of all.

A Leap Into Love

A Sweet Regence Romance Novella, a sequel to
The Marquess and the Midwife

Can a gentleman be too charming?
The ladies of Upper Upton think so.
When the single ladies of the village conspire to teach their charmer a lesson that might bankrupt him, the town's loveliest young widow—who's sworn off marriage forever—steps up to warn him.

Liliana's Letter

Finalist, 2015 National Reader's Choice Award

The Matchmaker Meets the Matchbreaker

Liliana Ashford's future as a professional chaperone depends on her wealthy charge's successful marriage, but her own close encounter with a scoundrel years ago makes her determined to save the girl from the same kind of rogue.

The Ghost of Depford Hall

A short, sweet Halloween story, a sequel to
Liliana's Letter

It's her mother's last All Hallows' Eve.
When family, friends, and tenants gather, goblins, ghouls, and ghosts are banned from this All Hallows' Eve party.
Only, no one told the Ghost of Depford Hall!

Courted by the Earl

Previously titled *Bella's Band*

A 2015 RONE Award Finalist

Saddled with his brother's title and debts, nothing about this new life makes the Earl of Hackwell want to stay—until he meets a lady with a secret that can change everything.

Rosalyn's Ring

2014 Book Buyer's Best Winner, Novella Category

Done with grieving her losses, a late nobleman's daughter has fallen into a tidy spinster's life in London. But when one snowy Christmas Eve, a young woman needs rescue, she seizes the chance to do good—and to recover a family heirloom that ought to be hers.

Haunting Miss Fenwick

Thrilled to finally have a permanent home, a Squire's daughter won't let a supernatural creature scare her away. While hunting the ghost she doesn't believe in, she stumbles upon a mysterious flesh and blood man who might be the key to all of her problems.

The Duke She Despised

Book 1 in the Upstart Christmas Brides Series

Hiding her true identity, a young vicar's widow takes a position as housekeeper in a remote Scottish castle at Christmas for a new duke who years ago sabotaged her chance for happiness. She quickly falls for the duke's charming but not very competent factor, not knowing that he's hiding something also—he's the duke she despised!

Convincing the Countess

Book 2 in the Upstart Christmas Brides Series

A business-minded aristocrat finds himself pursuing a casual affair with a widowed countess...until love changes everything.

The Impetuous Heiress

Book 3 in the Upstart Christmas Brides Series

Before dashing Lord Loughton can make amends with his neglected fiancée, the lady's meddling cousin delivers her to his doorstep. He soon realizes more is amiss than his carelessness. Can he uncover her secrets and win her back before he loses her altogether?

Available in Spring 2022

The Macbeth Series

Fated Hearts

A Love After All Retelling of the Scottish Play

A Scottish Baron returning from two decades at war meets the wife he divorced and the daughter he disavowed before she was born, only to learn that everything he'd believed was a lie. Determined to win back the only woman he's ever loved he must first face the viper who drove them apart.

The Comtesse of Midnight

A Scottish Earl on a quest for the elusive Comtesse de Fontenay, rescues a French lady smuggler during a devastating storm, taking shelter with her. As the stormy night drags on, he suspects she knows the lady he's seeking, the lady who holds the secret to his identity.

Claims of the Heart

Since a perilous fall, Lucie Macbeth has been seeing more than a settled future as the heiress to a Scottish barony. The visions plaguing her include a man—one far above her class and breeding, and English to boot. He's engaged to a duke's granddaughter as well, and thus wholly inappropriate. Though she can't marry him, and she won't become any man's leman, when the Sight warns her of danger to him her conscience, and her heart tell her she can't walk away.

Available in Spring 2022

Find out more at
https://AlinaKFiield.com
and sign up for my monthly emails for news about upcoming books and sales.

www.ingramcontent.com/pod-product-compliance
Lightning Source LLC
LaVergne TN
LVHW010103110826
845155LV00028B/460

* 9 7 8 1 9 4 4 0 6 3 3 4 4 *